LOVE
SHOOK
MY
HEART

LOVE SHOOK MY HEART

Edited by Irene Zahava

alyson
books

LOS ANGELES • NEW YORK

Manufactured in the United States of America.

This trade paperback original is published by Alyson Publications Inc.,
P.O. Box 4371, Los Angeles, California 90078-4371.
Distribution in the United Kingdom by Turnaround Publisher Services Ltd.,
Unit 3 Olympia Trading Estate, Coburg Road, Wood Green,
London N22 6TZ England.

First edition: February 1998

02 01 00 99 98   10 9 8 7 6 5 4 3 2 1

ISBN 1-55583-404-3

Library of Congress Cataloging-in-Publication Data
    Love shook my heart / edited by Irene Zahava. — 1st ed.
        ISBN 1-55583-404-3
        1. Lesbians—Fiction. 2. Short stories, American—Women authors.
    3. Lesbians' writings, American. 4. Love stories, American.
    I. Zahava, Irene.
    PS648.L47L68 1998
    813'.01089206643—dc21   97-32629 CIP

Credits
    "Muffie's Midnite Lounge, 1958," by Cathy Cockrell, is excerpted from a
novel in progress.
    "Baby Pictures," by Martha Clark Cummings, first appeared in *Hurricane
Alice,* Volume 5, Number 1, 1988.
    "Becca and the Woman Prince," by Carolyn Gage, first appeared in *From the
Flames* (Nottingham, England), Summer 1996.
    "First Love at Sweet Briar," by Sally Miller Gearhart, first appeared in *The
New Our Right to Love: A Lesbian Resource Book,* edited by Ginny Vida. New
York: Simon & Schuster, 1996. Reprinted by permission of the author.
    "In Case of Emergency," by Anndee Hochman, first appeared in *Boston Re-
view,* April/May 1997.
    "The Common Price of Passion," by Jess Wells, is excerpted from a novel of
the same title.

Love shook my heart
like the mountain wind
rushing through the trees.

—SAPPHO

For Martha Blue Waters
because you shake my heart

Contents

Switch

by
Carol Guess

For several years I lived with a small olive-skinned woman named Jo, who passed as a man at the brake factory where she worked. The factory was six blocks from our house; very often I'd walk with her in the mornings, carrying her lunch in a wide gray box, holding an umbrella (for it rained more often in those days), and stopping once or twice on the way to kiss. The men who worked Jo's shift knew my name, and when they saw us saying good-bye at the corner, they'd heckle Jo good-naturedly. It amazes me now to think it, but we were never found out, and after the first year or so, we began to take the men's comments for granted, to believe in them ourselves, to believe that we were assured a place in their particular order.

We fought often, Jo and I, often and hard; but our fights were always contained within our walls. On the street, in the diner where I worked, and in front of the factory we were unified, not because we felt the need to perform but because our fights were always relative: Outside it was still us against them. And always, always our fights ended with the same threat: with Jo running her hands through my long hair, saying, "Don't you cut this, Caddie. Don't you change this." What there was between us — electricity and patience — traveled the bridge of my reddish black hair. My feminine exterior made her invisible as a woman even as it thrilled her. Wrapping her fingers around the nape of my skull, she'd say "Don't you change this, Caddie. Caddie, don't you change."

She left me the night of our third winter's first real frost. She must've taken her things and burdened them on her shoulders; when I woke, the frost was settled in for four good months, and she was gone.

I watched at the factory door for her small self, but she never appeared, and after a week I dared enter the office: the first time I'd ever been inside the factory. The narrow woman behind the battered desk put down the phone long enough to tell me Jo had quit — not the day she'd left me but two weeks before. I tried counting the ways we'd made love those fourteen days and felt sick and foreign inside myself, as if I were pregnant.

The frost stayed and stayed, and each night I imagined her soft half smile and her harsh laugh, and the cold got beneath my skin and lodged, past the help of any fire.

With spring I grew restless and moved into an apartment closer to town. The two small rooms felt alternately cramped and vacant; the walls were crosshatched with other people's scratches. I hung a photo of Jo on the wall of the second room, but her face loomed like some terrible Jesus and spoke to me like the Goose Girl's Falada. So I took it down and played music so loudly and consistently that I was evicted.

I moved across the street to a second-floor apartment, whose sunny windows meant nothing to me. In between my shifts at the diner I slept, never dreaming but always wanting to, sometimes waking up with the taste of Jo's skin on my lips, as if my mouth had a memory.

Because Jo was the first person to say that she loved me, I did not know who I was now. I tried talking to other people, but all I wanted to discuss was passion, so I stayed quiet. I had nothing to help me decipher the world around me or to understand what it meant that I wanted no part of it.

I did not know where to go.

I had met Jo by accident, known her for a woman and wondered. We had met by chance, but now I couldn't rely on chance. I knew there were others like us because Jo had told stories. She'd been in love and had been loved before. So, yes, there were others, and I knew in my blood that there were others. But where — I didn't know that. I kept my eyes open, that was all.

After Jo for a while there was David. The first day he appeared in the diner, I stood over him to take his order, and he hung his head like some shy horse. I liked the way his black hair lay ragged just above his collar, and I somehow knew even before he showed his face that he would look like Jo; the surprise was only that he looked more like Jo than himself. He courted me hard, and he might have taken me far away from Martinsville, Indiana, to one of the cold Northern states he talked about often. I could've had fat babies and a house with a garage.

But kissing David wasn't like kissing Jo. He would press me against his pickup, fumble with my shirt, grab my nipples with hands curled almost into fists. I liked the feel of his hip against mine, but my breasts hurt, and his tongue moved too fast. Kissing David wasn't like kissing Jo. The difference can be easily explained, but not here or now. Let me say simply that he lacked some things and had an overabundance of others, by which I don't mean what you think but something altogether different. Let me say simply that he moved on, taking a young girl with him, and that I stayed, to serve coffee and the $1.99 special to the regulars, six days a week, 6 A.M. to 4 P.M.

Maybe eight months went by after David. Some things inside me closed; at first I worried that they'd never open back up, but after a time I stopped worrying and began to accept the shutdown feeling. I looked at neither women nor men, neither left nor right as I walked to work. When I ate my dinner, I sat by myself in front of my window or in the corner of the diner after I finished

Switch

my shift, reading magazines full of recipes, full of
pictures of England's princess and hints on how to
please a husband once you had one. I sat alone,
and the regulars knew me well enough to know I
wanted it that way. I felt myself going gradually to
ice, but I couldn't stop it and wasn't sure I wanted
to. It seemed necessary. Most folks knew about Jo,
so I had sympathy: They'd say, "Her man left her."
So I was safe and cold and well-fed in Martinsville, Indiana, and I did not imagine my life
switching gears.

The owners of the diner, Marv and Helen, hired
their girls carefully, knowing that a good waitress
keeps customers better than good food. Selena
was the pretty one: flirty and sassy, still single,
serving up hope with each order. Bet was the
steady one, calm and attentive; the regulars chose
Bet's tables when they were tired or needed their
food done quick. Picky eaters chose Bet. And me?
I was the listener. I got the religious fanatics and
the hard-up and the angry young men who planned
to leave someday for Indy. We balanced out, but
Marv and Helen thought there was room for another. So one day they hung up a sign, and for over
a week we had girls streaming in and out, a regular pageant, almost as good for business as the
spring tractor pull.

Me and Selena and Bet watched the parade skep-
tically. We wanted to be sure there was no duplica-
tion. She had to be different, not competition but

complement, someone we could rely on but shove around a little at first, someone who wouldn't break but not a tough girl.

When Gwen walked in, Bet nudged me, and Selena pointed: They knew. And when I saw her, I knew too. Gwen would be the sweet one, the one to giggle, nod shyly, and occasionally fumble, serving Tom Jensen the cherry instead of the blueberry-walnut pie. We all three conferred, and I walked in back to tell Marv we'd spotted her, that she was Gwen, and that she was to be the girleen among us.

She started working that week. At twenty-one she was pretty in a childish way, round face pale and cheerful, gold hair to her waist, brown eyes set slightly too far apart for beauty. When she laughed she covered her mouth with her right hand: She had buck teeth and hated her own smiles. Her dresses were handmade, pinks and blues, small flowers pulled around her waist in simple stitches. "Gwennie," the factory men called her, and the name stuck. She looked young and simple, but she wasn't stupid. She earned her tips, flirting in her own shy and awkward way, acting the part of someone slightly more naive and cheerful than she really was. She could've been a threat to all of us, but instead she deferred; used to older sisters, she gave us the better tables, pressed her back against the counter when we needed to pass with trays of food, and waited to use the register.

Switch

Some weeks after Gwen first started working, there was an odd morning rush: Suddenly there was a line to sit, and everyone was short-tempered and hurried. Even Arthur Parks, a calm, decent man who tipped well and never asked for refills, sounded impatient. Things didn't calm down until 10:30, when the place cleared out as suddenly as it had filled. As the last of the factory men filed through the back exit, the front door jangled, and Cory Flint walked in, just off from the 2-to-10 shift at the bank where he worked as a watchman. As I served Cory his hash browns, he motioned toward Gwen.

"New girl?" he asked, and I nodded. "She looks too young to be feeding strangers."

"Better than feeding a strange man of her own," I sassed back, and he grinned for the first time that morning. Then he looked down at the blue-rimmed plate I'd set before him.

"She sure is a pretty one," he said as he unrolled his fork and spoon and knife from inside a paper napkin. "Sure has some pretty dress on, with flowers scattered all unusual like, up around her waist." I watched as he cut his fried ham into little triangles. "Sure has some pretty field of flowers on, that's right."

I turned his coffee cup upright and filled it silently, then walked back behind the counter, where Gwen and Bobby, the day cook, were looking over a newspaper someone had left behind.

"I'm going back to catch a smoke," I said to neither one of them in particular. "Call me if someone hits one of my tables."

Out back on the stoop, I held a cigarette between my fingers, wanting only the feel of it, not the taste or the heat. The sky was cloudy with factory smoke, but for once it didn't bother me; I watched the blackish coils go gray, then fade into the dirty expanse of sky. To my left a huge cross rose up from the Baptist church; to my right cars drove steadily through the drive-up automatic banking machine. I thought for a second about Jo, how she'd loved cars, her fascination with anything that meant easy motion.

I stood up and dusted off my skirt, but as I pulled the belt straight around my waist, I felt something close over me, and without wanting to I shut my eyes and put my hand to my lips, imagining that I was standing in our old orange kitchen while Jo knelt down in front of me, her hands on my hips, my hands on her head, her eyes buried inside me. When Gwen put her hand on my shoulder, I jumped.

"You've got a man," she said, "table five. Not like a regular."

I tossed my unlit cigarette into the grass and followed her inside.

That night I dreamed about Gwen. I woke long before my alarm and sat up in bed awhile, my arms wrapped around my knees, listening to the clock as it toyed with its minutes. The sky outside was black, cut with stars that looked close but that I knew to be unreachable. Then I got up, slipped on my robe, and pulled a book from the nightstand. In the kitchen I cut myself a piece of pie and put on water for tea. Opening the book, I read: "In the beginning...."

I read for two hours, until it was time to dress for work. I made myself read out loud, without stopping, because I felt dirty and dizzy with what I'd seen myself do. Gwen wasn't Jo; I knew that much. Gwen had long hair like me; she wore dresses and heels and flirted with the men from the factory. Gwen had a beau; I'd seen them kiss in the lot mornings before work. Gwen was a woman. I didn't know what wanting her would make me.

All day at work I broke things: plates empty and full, coffee cups, saucers gray with the ash of men's stubbed cigarettes.

At around 3 Bobby came up behind me and tugged on the knot of my apron.

"Yo, honey pie. Marv's got a note out for ya," he said, but I brushed him off and stomped into the kitchen, where Marv was flipping burgers on the grill.

"Caddie, seems like something might be bothering you. Seems like you probably aren't running up our china bill just because. You gonna tell me what that something is? Or you gonna tell me, maybe, that it's none of Marv's business but that you'll handle those plates a ways better next time, huh?" Marv didn't look at me while he spoke but watched the meat carefully, tilting his head, scraping at the grill with a spatula.

I rubbed my nose. I liked Marv; he'd been kind to me all the five years I'd worked at the diner. I knew he wanted me to tell him something he could understand and fix. But what to say?

"Marv," I imagined myself saying to the tiny man bent over a row of frozen burgers, "Marv, my man Jo was really someone's Josephine. And now this Gwen we've got, well, I've taken to dreaming about kissing her. I think I'm in love with her. And I've been saying my Bible to scare it out of me, but I'm afraid that hasn't done anything but make me more curious about her little flowered dress."

Thinking this way, I laughed, and even with Marv's surprised face turned toward me, I just couldn't stop laughing. My mouth stayed open and sound came out, sound like something tangled unwinding, sweet and jagged at once, out of place, unstoppable.

Waiting for Marianne

by

Harlyn G. Aizley

After Marianne decided she didn't want to be involved with me, I went crazy. Not suddenly. But later. And slowly. So that I didn't even know I had slipped over the edge of sanity until I heard this song a few months into it that reminded me of her and how much I had wanted her and how much she had hurt me and how I totally had checked out since the day she said it wasn't going to work.

I don't know how to say this part, because it really sucks. But by the time I realized I had gone crazy in response to having fallen in love — or something — with Marianne, well, by that time I was already involved with somebody else. Shit. You know what I mean.

That's why I went to Utah. It was my birthday anyway, and I needed something big to happen, so I packed my bags and flew west just like in the movies. Carol, my new girlfriend, was not too pleased to see me go, but there was nothing she could do to get me to change my mind. I didn't want to lose her, but I wasn't with her like I should have been. For all that we shared, my heart was still hanging on to Marianne. I knew I had to stop listening to that song. I knew that if I stuck around any longer, I would wind up calling Marianne even though she had told me not to. That's why I left. It was my birthday anyway, time for something major to ring in the new year.

I had been on the road for a week when I met Nan and her granddaughter, Meg.

"Nan Perkins, escapee from southern Indiana, just north of the Kentucky border. Pleased to meet you!" This was her introduction as I sat numb and strange at a picnic table in a campground at Zion National Park.

I had remembered everything except the tent and was sleeping each night in my rented car until Nan found me and decided to save my life. She wandered over one morning with a cup of coffee and announced that I was the talk of the town, sleeping in an Escort with the seats back and cooking hot dogs on a stick.

"No tent, no friends, and no items," Nan delivered her assessment that morning after handing me what seemed like the best cup of coffee I ever had tasted. "Looks to me like you ran away."

I tried to tell her that, in fact, I was on a planned and well-thought-out vacation but failed to convince either her or myself.

"Guess I needed to get away in a hurry," I finally conceded.

"What happened, you knock somebody up?" Nan laughed so hard, she had to spit out a mouthful of Dark French Roast, sent dutifully by her sister all the way from Chicago.

"I wish," I said, thinking that even that, a little girl-to-girl parthenogenesis, would be better than this, running away to break somebody's heart, which I now knew I was destined to do as soon as I returned home, because life on the lam had convinced me that it was over with Carol. "I need to break up with someone who loves me because I'm hopelessly in love with someone who doesn't."

"Ah," Nan said, looking me up and down. "I should have known."

I didn't meet Meg until later that afternoon. She was out hanging clothes from a long red cord she had tied to two piñon trees in back of their RV. I honestly was not in search of friendship — I really, truly just wanted to lie around and feel sorry for myself — but they loaned me a tent and invited me to dinner, took me hiking up to the emerald pools.

One night by a campfire, I spilled my guts. I told them how Marianne wouldn't see me, how Carol wouldn't let go. They both listened and poked at embers with the long green branches we had found earlier by a stream. "Perfect!" Nan had announced when Meg and I handed her our three favorites. "Absolutely splendid." She stroked each one as a tailor would yards of the finest silk.

"Seems a shame," Nan said now, sifting thoughtfully through the dying flames, "with all the love in the world, to go around chasing after your own tail."

I wasn't sure what she meant but thought it big and profound and later wrote it down in my journal by flashlight when I was alone in the tent. I was grateful for the shelter, for room enough to stretch out my legs, for the mesh skylight through which I could watch the stars at night and ponder such things as love and lust and Marianne.

Illuminating small pockets of the night sky with my flashlight, I sketched the stars above and remembered the evening Marianne and I first kissed, how she drew us into a pentangle she had etched into the wet sand.

"For good luck," she had said as we held each other tight.

All it had taken to fall helplessly in love were those soft kisses, shooting stars falling into the ocean, and the pentangle on the shore. Back in the city Marianne kissed me again, looked into my eyes, and told me she probably wouldn't call for several days.

"Why not?" I asked. Already losing ground.

"Because I'm going to go home and freak out."

Marianne really couldn't help what happened to her when she fell in love or got too close. Once, after spending the weekend with someone, she had gone home and thrown up. Marianne was not just afraid of intimacy, she was allergic to it.

I turned off the flashlight and saw in the passing clouds all of the conversations until dawn, endless wondering about whether or not to keep trying, painful hours and sometimes days of waiting. Always waiting for Marianne.

Thankfully, Meg came by early the next day to ask if I wanted to join her on a hike.

"There's this trail that leads down the river. I mean *in* the river if that's okay with you."

It was fine, of course, because Meg was beautiful and because even earlier that morning, after a long night of contemplation, I had broken up with Carol on the phone, which is a terrible thing to do, I know, but I just couldn't help it. Once you start with "We need to talk when I get back," it's basically over.

"Just say it, Cass." Carol kind of both pleaded and yelled so that I felt guilty and mad all at the same time.

"Say what?"

"That you want to break up."

I wanted to say, "But I don't," but knew better and instead fell silent.

"Come on, Cass. It's not fair for me to do it when you're the one who wants it to end."

"I'm sorry" was all I could say.

"Me too," she said and hung up.

Carol was the nurse who had kept me alive, a rebound to prevent me from drowning in leftover passion, someone to receive all of the abandoned kisses welling up inside. These crazy days in Utah were, I presumed, my first awkward steps alone, supported at last by nothing but the acknowledgment of sorrow. I was learning to walk again. But I had used somebody. I felt terrible and free.

"It ended pretty badly," I told Meg as we applied sunblock and grabbed bottles of water from Nan's refrigerator.

"Doesn't it always."

Nan was off that day on a date with this guy from Texas named Brodie. He used to RV every summer with his wife, but she had died a few years back, and this was his first time out alone. They were going fishing, and we were instructed to be back promptly at 6 for a fish fry.

Meg had a detailed map of the Virgin River and the narrows it led through; she also had a compass in her back pocket. We started by winding around the east wall of the canyon, along an easy one-mile trail that began at an amphitheater proudly named the Temple of Sinawava and ended at the gateway to the narrows, our river entry point. Along the way algae and ferns with delicate green tendrils grew as if by magic out of damp sandstone walls. Wildflowers with names like scarlet monkey and shooting star, and cactus flowers named after paintbrushes, all blossomed from the moist stone.

Meg insisted we hike to a platform she remembered about a mile down, and so we spent the next hour slogging carefully over moss-covered stone, watching as the gorge became darker and deeper. Once we were in the narrows, sandstone walls as tall as skyscrapers towered above us on either side, and our trail, the river itself, was about the width of the halls in my old high school. The platform, a welcome sight over an hour later, was a ledge of stone jutting out from the canyon wall, hanging like box seats three feet above the river. We hoisted ourselves up, unpacked the food we had brought along — cheese and bread and macaroons Nan had picked up in town — pulled off our soggy sneakers to dry, and sat back against the cool stone.

I was trying not to have a crush on Meg if only because it seemed so much like the thing to do, and I was a rebel now, after all, alone and free in Utah, heartsick for the unattainable. I played it cool and pretended not to care when she told me all about her mother and stepfather, her two brothers out in California, and her love affairs in college. I kept talking about Marianne and then softened a bit and told her about my family, how my parents had divorced after thirty-three years of marriage and how my sister had left her quiet life as a preschool teacher to try to become an aspiring actress in L.A.

Meg told me she designed gardens for a living. And I told her I took art classes at night as I tried to decide what to do with my life by day. We saw two herons and an egret, watched the sun make its slow journey across the only visible sliver of sky, and compared tattoos. We talked about haircuts and jobs and movies we had seen. And just as I was convincing myself it was all right to enjoy this, that it was neither tacky nor trite to have a crush on the most obvious girl in the most likely of circumstances, Meg looked down at her watch and announced it was time to head back.

Alas, I thought and packed up my pencils and paper as well as my heart, put on a pair of damp sneakers, and leapt from the ledge to land beside Meg, who stood already smiling in the water below.

"Be careful," she said as we raced the twilight, plummeted between stones, and dodged mini-rapids, catching ourselves in time to avoid falls into the icy water.

From a safe distance I was thinking about lust, about the way two people fall in love, about sand-stone and charcoal and burnt sienna. Meg up ahead led the way like a storm trooper or some sexy den mother, shouting out warnings of slippery areas, protruding branches and stones. I watched as she danced through the water, tried to picture her home, the gardens she grew.

Behind me the view was dark and cavernous like the mouth of a great big monster, the sandstone towers its jagged jaws, the river its long wet tongue we were racing. I looked back once and shuddered aloud.

"Scared?" Meg turned and smiled.

"Of course not."

She laughed. And then, as we continued on our messy trot, she suddenly asked, "Hey, Cass, who do you fall in love with? I mean, what type of people do you go crazy over? Because I've got a sort of theory."

The rushing river seemed quite a place for a theory on love. "What's your theory?"

"Tell me who first."

"Okay." I thought back. "The ones I was nuts over?"

"Them," she said ominously.

"Well, Rebecca was a photographer. And crazy Jane was a writer. Simon, the guy I went out with in high school, was a painter. Marianne is a pianist—"

"Aha!" Meg shouted without turning her head.

"Aha what?" I called out after her.

"What about you?"

"What about me?"

"Who are you?"

"Confused."

"No, think about it," she persisted. "You keep thinking you need to find something to do with your life. You can't decide whether or not to be a doctor or a lawyer. But I see you. You spend all of your time drawing."

"So…"

"So you fall in love with artists because you're looking for that part of yourself," Meg said, still forging ahead.

I didn't feel like crying, but my eyes began to fill with tears.

"That desperate longing that seems so much larger than life, for Marianne or anyone else, you know, like this love will bring together earth and sky." She splashed around greatly in her earnestness. "It's for a part of yourself. Nobody else is worth all that. Believe me."

I stopped dead in my wet tracks.

Undaunted, Meg stopped and turned to me. "Don't force yourself to go to graduate school, Cass, just because you think you should, because it's safer. Be an artist. It's okay. It will help you to choose the right lovers."

I was just out-and-out crying by then. For reasons I couldn't explain. I suppose at that moment it seemed to me that my whole confused life of lust and indecision was revealed as a scrambled quest for freedom, for permission to be myself, like coming out or needing to sketch everything I saw. I know it sounds impossible, but with a quick and dramatic flash, Marianne and all the others slipped away like looming backdrops suddenly reduced to life-size props behind the magic curtain, faded at last into the deep red sandstone that surrounded me. Who would I be without them? If I truly set myself free?

"I'm sorry," Meg said, gently touching my hair. "I didn't mean to upset you."

"It's okay," I murmured.

"Listen, just don't give it all away. Save some for yourself, you know, that energy. Save some for me," she said, taking my hand.

And thus we walked home along the Virgin River bed, letting go only upon our arrival at the gateway to the narrows, through which we emerged like two charmed Alices from the other side of the looking glass.

I expected to feel even crazier than before but instead felt surprisingly sane. Meg was up ahead again, pointing out star formations, bats, and night lizards. I was tagging behind, carrying my pack, no strings attached, free at last, eyes wide open like never before. Meg bent to pick up a stone, held it up to me, and smiled.

Fifteen minutes had gone by. Fifteen minutes since we picked up the dry trail and headed for home. Fifteen minutes since Meg's gift of revelation. Fifteen minutes since she had released my hand as easily as she had taken it. Fifteen minutes. The first fifteen minutes in five-and-a-half months that I had not thought of Marianne.

It was past 6:30 when we stumbled in. From across the campground Nan shouted a rather frantic yet cheerful "Hi, girls! Hurry up, dinner's on the grill." She was bustling about, a spatula in one hand, a beer in the other. Sprawled out on a lawn chair was a big old cowboy, complete with pointed steel-toed boots, a Stetson with a feather train, and an enormous silver-and-turquoise belt buckle.

"Hi, Brodie," Meg called.

The cowboy stood from his chair and opened his arms wide. "Hey there, beautiful," he said as he scooped Meg up into a hug so big, it made me envious.

"You must be Cassie," he said to me and offered an embrace only slightly less intense than the one delivered to Meg. "Brodie Carlson. Pleased to meet ya."

"Hi, Brodie," I said, craning my neck to see his big red face, wide grin, and long gray hair. He even had on a bolo tie.

"Welcome back, and I hope you like trout. Nan here almost had a possum, damn near tore the place down looking for y'all."

I figured "having a possum" was the Texas cowboy equivalent of "running around like a chicken with its head cut off" back in New York.

"I'm sorry," I said for the second time that day.

Nan and Meg had exchanged kisses and were in deep debate over the pros and cons of adding garlic bread to the meal, so I assumed the possum was over and excused myself to the tent to change as well as to process the day's many and miraculous events.

Suffice it to say, I came to think of Meg as an angel, not in white but browns and reds, deep colors that seep out from the earth, rise like trees from the tall grass to kiss you gently like the breeze and free you from yourself. Intoxicated, we spent the next several days floating on a cloud of piñon and juniper, hiking to the farthest of the emerald pools nestled deep into the mountains, bathing beneath sandstone chaperons, and then lying back on the sand to watch the sun pass across the sky. We'd return each evening to Nan, who greeted us with a story and dinner, and then slip away to our private netherworlds, me to the tent and Meg to the RV. There I would lie back to watch the stars, the moon, and the faint memories of clouds. Some nights I swore I could hear her breathing, soft kisses next to me, breath as sweet and fragile as the columbine and maidenhair that clung impossibly to the trees and stones. The next morning I would wake to the smell of coffee, to the sound of children scrambling in and out of tents, or to Meg herself peeking in and coaxing me out for another day.

Back home they probably have twelve-step programs to wean you of such things, peace and lust and the trees and stars, forgetting and contentment. Sometimes Brodie would join us for dinner, he and Nan having spent the day fishing or shopping or smoking cigars. Nan was the first woman I ever met who smoked cigars, and once Meg and I brought one of her fat stogies with us but wound up coughing so much that the tender spell that embraced us was almost broken. We purged ourselves of the bitter smoke by dipping into that day's pool, taking three deep breaths, and slipping underwater. Beneath the surface, in another world with different rules, we held hands again, the first time since the river, opened our eyes to the crystal-green distortion, hair standing on end as if trying to pull us back to the surface, and kissed, a strange underwater kiss, neither here nor there, short nor long, before squeezing each other's hands and coming up for air. That day we held hands as we lay next to each other watching herons and egrets sail across the sky. That day, thanks to the coarse smoke of a grandmother's cigar, everything changed.

"Why don't you two tell an old lady just what the heck is goin' on," Nan said when greeting us that evening. Luckily, Brodie was either off in his own RV or fishing or playing cards with the other retirees.

Despite all of the time we spent together, the long days in the sun, hiking and swimming and sketching the views, Meg and I had not yet discussed just what the heck was going on. We still were talking of just about everything else, life and death, time and money, more theories on love and hate and everything in between. Meg taught me about flowers and rainfall, and I showed her how to draw with pastels. We had covered travel, therapy, and the wonders of clumping kitty litter, but we had not touched upon the topic of us. It didn't seem necessary. We simply were living whatever it was that we were doing.

So imagine my surprise when Meg responded, "We're in love."

Nan must have noticed the look on my face, a combination of shock, excitement, and disbelief. I thought Meg was joking, a too-close-to-home, boy-that-sure-didn't-go-over-as-I-had-planned kind of thing.

"Well, darlin', that's fine with me, but it looks like it's news to Cassie here."

But Meg had left the conversation, thrown down her pack, and gone inside the RV. I looked imploringly toward the miniature screen door.

"Why don't you go on in?" Nan offered. "I've got some business to take care of over at the rangers' station."

Nan was smooth, could glide in and out of any situation without casting so much as a shadow. I waited until she was a few sites over, already engaged in a dynamic conversation with a couple from Missouri, and then went inside.

Meg had fixed us two tall glasses of iced tea and was just standing there looking toward the door, waiting.

"We're in love?"

"I am."

"With me?"

"No, Cass, with the Escort. I've always wanted to sleep in a car."

"Wow."

"What about you?"

What about me? It was a good question. I had just learned my own name, had lost myself the past few days, surrendered to the moment, to the beginning of each day as the entrance into a new world. I even had stopped thinking about Marianne, was just living in a tent, hanging out with someone named Meg, a year younger than myself and traveling around with her grandmother. We had held hands a couple of times, and when we did, my heart ignited. But then we'd settle back into our separate spaces, drawing and writing and telling our tales. I looked forward to every new day with her and conveniently had not considered anything more, life beyond Zion National Park. Though one day I did call my boss and beg for more time off.

"Can you really know you love someone so soon?" That was not what I'd meant to say. What I had really meant to say was something like, "Look, I've experienced love at first sight only once in my life, and it screwed me. I don't even know what love is anymore. I was involved with someone the past four months, and I told her that I loved her, all the while knowing that I didn't. She needed to hear it, and for some reason I needed to think I felt it. The only person I think I love is this image inside my head of someone I used to know — or maybe even wanted to be — who hurt me so bad, I went crazy and left home for Utah of all places."

"Yes," Meg said. She looked so small and serious, wiry, with hair the color of sand. "Yes, I do believe in love at first sight."

The glasses in her hands actually began to tremble, just like in the movies. I took them from her and laid them to rest on the nearest table. All that I thought I should be saying and all that I wanted to say canceled each other out and left me speechless, silent before Meg, shaken but holding strong. It was easier for me to look at the glasses than into those eyes, which for the first time I noticed were the same color as her hair, matched the smell of coconut and spice that engulfed her — or so I realized finally and at long last. That it had been not just the pygmy pine, cottonwood, and box elder that had found its way under my skin and into my heart; not just the slickrock paintbrush, lizards and Gambel quail, the roadrunners and occasional golden eagle but Meg herself, my guide and spirit, my teacher and companion of the last few days, my stranger and my confidante.

"To be able to love is the very best thing," I said, sounding like some creature from *Winnie-the-Pooh,* "but I think I'm wounded still and learning. The doors are all closed."

"I can wait." Meg stepped toward me and reached out her hands, drawing me in. Lock and key. Always and forever.

We spent that night together in the tent. Nan continued to be the world's grandest diplomat, fetching Brodie and driving off to town so Meg wouldn't feel guilty about stealing a night away.

"All I want is for my kids to be happy, to know what it's like to love and be loved. It's a crazy stinkin' world, Brodie. Every kiss heals the earth."

Brodie, new to the idea of two girls in love, let Nan drive and do the talking.

The forwarded mail, delivered to my picnic table earlier in the day, was left unopened; the birthday cards, student loan notices, handwritten farewell letter from Carol, even a card from Marianne piled up on the front seat of the car as Meg and I lay in each other's arms counting the stars and clouds above, dreaming our dreams, and looking toward tomorrow.

At Frank's

by

Tzivia Gover

There was something I'd been meaning to do, and oddly, sitting here across from Whit at Frank's Miniature Hot Dogs in Topsfield, I figured the time seemed right.

Whit used to work in Topsfield, installing solar hot water systems, and as we drove through the neighborhoods of little ranches and capes, we saw some of her handiwork on the rooftops: slanting panels like sliding boards gaping southward to catch the sun. That tangle of streets holds memories for her. We were driving out of the residential neighborhoods and onto a highway lined with corrugated metal buildings and automotive stores. That's when she mentioned Frank's.

"Let's go there now," I said, happy to be riding through her past, a place that seemed to make her grow calm.

Inside Frank's is a dark wood bar lined with red vinyl stools, booths with pockmarked tabletops, and an adjacent family dining room where the television is on.

Above the bar there is a series of paper American flags with names written across them in thick black letters. We don't know what Fourth of July ritual has produced these banners, but they indicate that here in Topsfield there is an in crowd of people with names like Pete and Betty and they believe in things like flags and bars.

I know that's a lot to draw from a couple of rows of paper flags hanging on a wall, but I get a strong sense of it in the dark depths of Frank's, where stubble-faced men in flannel shirts hover over tables beneath the dartboard.

I tune all of this out and try to believe in the friendliness of our waitress, who takes our order before we see a menu. Whit asks for five mini hot dogs (two for me and three for her) with everything on them and two ginger ales.

I asked her to order. It is part of a fantasy I'm in. We're at Frank's, and she's my guy, and she is as tough as the men in back. I know so because in this scene I have created, we all grew up together, and she's beaten them up after football practice once or twice. I'm her girl, and we're as regular as daytime television.

Whit bites into her mini frank, which is less than four inches long, thin as a finger, and nestled into a tiny bun. "It pops when you bite it," she says.

I sink my teeth into my own, and it does pop, like cracking open a beer.

I'm leaving soon for graduate school, and our life together is going to change. I've decided to give Whit my pinkie ring. Actually it's my mother's college ring, and I've taken it to the jewelers to have my initials engraved behind the onyx seal stone. I even asked my mother for her blessing before giving it away. It is the closest thing I have to a family heirloom, after all. My mother gave it to me on the day of my sister's wedding, kind of like a consolation prize, I guess.

"See if it fits," I say, passing the ring across the table.

"Why?" Whit asks, hopeful.

"I want you to wear it while I'm gone." Her palm is open, and my fingers are hovering above. I gently drop the ring into her waiting hand. The tension the moment holds is like that of a suspension bridge, providing a link across a great distance. This moment is one to savor quickly, because we are in Frank's trying to be two girlfriends on a break from their husbands in the eyes of the waitresses and the guys drinking beer farther back.

And at the same time I'm in my '50s movie: Sandra Dee and Sal Mineo — and my college seal ring is in the air between us.

And at the same time we are two lesbians doing something we shouldn't be doing in public.

Whit's fingers curl around the ring, embracing my gesture.

"Like it?" I ask.

She nods, letting her lips smile a little. I direct her to look at the inscription on the band. A detached expression floats across the surface of her face. She's trying to look like she is squinting to find a scratch or something. She is trying to look like nothing is really going on here, at our table at Frank's. But I see excitement skip through her fingers as she slips on the ring.

"Which finger?" she asks.

"Any one," I say, watching her settle the band onto the ring finger of her left hand.

"Just right," she says, giving her hand a little shake.

I smile, satisfied. Then my hand, working without my consent, reaches out and takes hold of hers.

"Not here," she says quietly.

"I know," I say and pull it back.

First Love at Sweet Briar

by

Sally Miller Gearhart

Daylight was fading, but from my desk by the window on the second floor of Randolph Hall, I could see Lakey begin stripping the moment she stepped off the Lynchburg bus. By the time she crossed the quadrangle and reached the arcade, she had removed her hat, replaced the hatpin, crammed her short gloves into her linen purse, and begun unbuttoning both her suit jacket and her blouse, all this while juggling an overburdened shopping bag. When she flung open the door to our room moments later, her feet were free of the linen pumps, and the waistband to her skirt was opened, the placket unzipped.

"I finally found the Ayn Rand," she announced, dumping shopping bag, hat, purse, jacket, and shoes on the bed, "but nobody had *Lost in the Stars.*"

Her monologue, fired by the intensity of her disrobing, ebbed and flowed with the range of resistance offered by her clothes. Her words sped with the sliding of her skirt to the floor and the shrugging off of the silk blouse. They stopped altogether as she stepped out of the skirt and lifted her slip so she could begin unhooking her nylons. Her discourse gathered speed again and volume as she stood first on one foot and then on the other, recklessly peeling the precious stockings down her legs, over her ankles and feet.

"I wound up getting Silly Putty for Bobby and a book for Arlene," she burbled, undoing her garter belt and whipping it out of her panties. She slowed perceptibly to separate the straps of her slip from the straps of her bra, pulling them down over her arms and sending the slip to the floor alongside her skirt. While she hoisted on her faded rolled-leg jeans, her voice rose again, and when she slid her bare feet into the run-down white penny loafers, she eased into her quiet ending.

"Lookie here!" She tossed me a small bag. "Cotton beauties. Five pair for a dollar."

She swung into the ample folds of her brother's cast-off shirt, leaving the tail to hang out mid-thigh over her jeans, and buttoned herself at last into a satisfied silence.

Thus, the proper vision of the Sweet Briar Girl, Girl of Grace and Beauty, Girl of Good Taste and Good Judgment, stood revested in the comfort of clothes that the college tolerated only in the privacy of dorm rooms or under the protection of long coats. She was beautiful, and I loved her.

I think now that we were both making a memory of that moment, Lakey standing there transfixed as our eyes met, me sitting there clutching a bag of white panties. We did that a lot — when we were alone, of course — looking at each other in breath-stilled silences, as if we understood in some part of ourselves that we could not hold the joy forever and that somewhere, ages and ages hence, we would need to believe again in the incredible fullness of all we were finding in each other.

Lakey broke the spell by diving into the shopping bag.

"Close your eyes and hold out your hands."

I did so. I could hear her move toward me. Then I felt her lean over me as the window shade spooled down and the desk light snapped off. *Not even a silhouette,* I thought. We'd learned to be so careful.

I waited. Then instead of some Shmoo doll or a box of tampons (latest craze for the "modern woman"), I felt her strong hands over mine, raising me to my feet. Softly, like a mother taking up a sleeping babe, she drew me into her arms. I rested my head on top of her shoulder. She buried her face in my neck. We stood holding each other, laughing softly and sighing in the sheer contentment of our full-body contact, rocking back and forth, there in the twilight of a Virginia springtime.

Her gift was Franck's Symphony in D Minor. We put its first record on the phonograph, turned the volume low, and set a straight chair casually against our lockless door — not to block it but to provide at least some flimsy obstacle, a second or two of warning in case some friend burst in upon us. Then we stretched out on our wide bed, made up of our two single beds thrust together — "to save space," we always explained to those who had the nerve to ask. We doused the lamp, prayed that no one would call us to the phone, and settled into each other's arms to listen and to love.

It was long past dinner, long past vespers, long past the 10-o'clock closing down of the campus when we emerged into the moonlight of the second-floor arcade. Two of our classmates sat on the single bench, smoking and huddled together against the night's chill. We knew they were holding hands beneath the light blanket that covered their knees. And we knew that in their room, two beds had been thrust together to make one large one. We knew, they knew we knew, we knew that they knew we knew, and we all worked tirelessly to avoid any acknowledgment of that knowing.

We returned their soft greeting and then leaned into our own separate conversation, speaking in low voices and lighting up Lakey's Chesterfield, my Pall Mall. We had homework to discuss, books to compare, papers to write.

It was 1951. We were suspended in an isolated pocket of leisure and privilege, far from the war stirring in Korea or the witch-hunts in Congress. We were third-year students at one of the nation's finest women's colleges, daily discovering vast new intellectual horizons, sounding the depths of astounding inner oceans of creativity. And in the spring of the previous year we had unexpectedly found in each other a passion that had almost blown our lives asunder.

My small rural "class C" high school had given me very little of the background necessary for admission to Sweet Briar, and it was not at all clear that I could handle even the first year of that college's courses. The admissions director allowed me to enter as a kind of experiment in "underprepared students."

It took me six weeks to discover that I was out of my intellectual league, out of my social class, and probably out of my mind. I found no friends, I could not communicate with my roommate, I understood little of what textbooks and professors said, I was appalled by the weekend dating frenzy, and I hated the food, which, moreover, had to be eaten at least twice a week in hose and heels. I'd never been so lonely, homesick, and miserable — before or since.

Two things saved me. First, the theater reached out and claimed me for her own. I was hooked by her timeless magic, and as I settled into roles for the winter and spring productions, my days became tolerable. Second, Lakey entered my life. On a warm afternoon on the steps of the dormitory, I was rolling up my jeans so they would not show beneath my raincoat. I bumped Lakey, also rolling up her jeans. We both grinned, apologized, and then began a conversation about one of her books that went on over coffee and hot-plate chili until 3 the following morning.

Throughout that spring and our following sophomore year, we spent time together almost every day. Since we dated only occasionally, we spent long weekends traipsing over the campus's hills and forests, exploring trails, bridle paths, and the beer joint two miles down the main highway. I was an unapologetic Galatea to Lakey's Pygmalion: an eager, unschooled, undisciplined diamond in the rough whose thirst for information and ideas must have astonished even her wise heart. With Lakey I discovered how to take a thesis apart and put it back together, how to listen to messages from myself that would take me into worlds I had never dreamed existed. I see her even now in my memory, flinging open door after intellectual door, leading me by the hand to treasure troves of history, music, and poetry.

When I discovered to my delight that Lakey could handle a football, we'd often fill the West Dell with whoops of joy as we perfected our passing. We sang a lot, laughed a lot, read to each other, indulged in highly competitive contests of mumblety-peg and bridge, sparred verbally with our professors and classmates, pounded out papers on our Underwoods, and studied all night in the smoking room. We exhausted our bodies on the hockey field and our minds in the library. I discovered how to organize my ideas and my time. Toward the end of my second year, it dawned on me that I was passing my courses with more than D's. And to boot I had Lakey and a growing circle of friends. I remember skipping to class one bleak rainy morning, alive with the new sweet knowledge that I was happy.

That school year, 1949–1950, Lakey and I each lived in a "single." Since each of us tired of having to trudge back to our own room after an evening of studying or talking, we planned to be roommates the following year. But for now, the night before we'd both be leaving for the summer, I stood in my room looking at the piled-up bed, covered with clothes, packing boxes, suitcases, books. Lakey had followed me down the hall.

"Leave it," she said, looking over my shoulder and then picking up my pillow. "Come sleep with me. We can squeeze together."

I nodded, exhausted and relieved.

We did our nightly libations, miraculously found our pajamas in the chaos of our packing, opened the window in hopes of some breeze, and fell into Lakey's narrow bed, dousing the light and covering ourselves only with a sheet. She faced the wall, and I lay inches from her so as not to crowd her or make the warm night more uncomfortable. I fitted my body into a shadow of her contours, not touching her and keeping my arms between us. She reached behind her to pat my buttocks good night. I patted her hand patting my buttocks, and then we each withdrew into our own bubble.

Sleep was not an option for me. I lay there suddenly aware of Lakey's body, its warmth and softness. I'd not allowed myself to think about how I would miss her over the summer. Our separation at Christmas and spring breaks hadn't been a problem. But now she was heading for Europe with her family, and I'd be with my summer stock company. We'd have an ocean between us.

Tears welled up inside me and began clogging my throat and nose. I tried to swallow softly and breathe evenly. A huge loneliness washed over me, a desolation. My life, which just yesterday had teemed with joy and excitement, was all at once dry, tasteless, meaningless. I didn't want her in Europe. I wanted her with me.

I risked a long, controlled inhalation, trying to hold back a sob. Then, as if bestowing a gift, my nose cleared, and I was drenched with the Johnson & Johnson shampoo smell of Lakey's hair. Some crazy notion entered my mind that at least I could carry that with me over the summer, the smell of her hair. I just wouldn't exhale, that's all. Just hold it in, right there inside me.

I was wondering if you could die holding your breath that way when a slow realization overtook me. Lakey wasn't breathing either. In fact, Lakey's body was tense, rigid, very much like my own. I held my breath for another eternity, not daring to disturb the silence. Then to my horror I felt my arm revving up to put itself around Lakey's waist. I mentally reprimanded it, only to feel it resist me. I focused on it, incredulous that it was disobeying me. But it was no longer my arm. It was somebody else's arm. Or just some dissociated independent member, hell-bent on reaching out now toward Lakey.

That rebellious arm never got to make its move. Instead, at that moment, Lakey's taut body began slowly turning, turning upward and around to face me and, without hesitation or haste, moving artlessly into my own waiting arms. The cry that was bursting from her and the release of my own explosive breath must surely have roused the whole sleeping quadrangle.

I understood with a clarity I've rarely experienced since then that my entire life up until that moment — every decision, every activity, every pain, every happiness — had been a preparation for that embrace. I was a wanderer at last come home, a skeleton at last enfleshed, an orchard at last in flower. I couldn't hold her tight enough. We lay shaking and crying and laughing in a delirium of release and joy, stunned and exuberant at what was happening, understanding it not at all, and incredulous that we had waited so long to express a love that now seemed so obvious and so total. Most of all we agonized with the knowledge that in a few hours, just having found each other, we would have to part.

There was no doubt that the energy between us was sexual, so far outdistancing any that we had ever felt with men that it was in another category altogether: intense, exhilarating, profound, and full of a million delicious possibilities. Yet we didn't touch each other genitally in any way. Instead we spent the night alternating between glory and peace, on the one hand kissing and stroking and tumbling in breathless excitement as we marveled at the new world that so suddenly had burst upon us, and on the other simply holding and rocking each other in a soft, sweet, newfound comfort. Nothing in Lakey's experience or in mine had prepared us for the power and meaning of that encounter.

As advertised, the summer was one long ache of missing each other and counting the days until we could return to Sweet Briar in the fall. Elizabeth and Essex, Antony and Cleopatra, Romeo and Juliet — their passion was a mere ember when set beside our reunion.

We arrived early, closed the door to our room, and barricaded it with heavy bureaus — we would explain that we were trying out various furniture arrangements. For two days we emerged from that room only to eat and use the bathroom. And even then, even with the breathless catching up and the all-over-again amazement at the depth and intensity of our feelings, even then we never touched each other sexually. In fact, we embarked on what I now am convinced was the longest sexual foreplay in the history of lesbianism. Maybe some unconscious sophistication was telling us, "Go slow, and the pleasure will be exponentially enhanced," or, since it was brand-new to us, maybe we were just plain scared.

Whatever the case, the time we spent together in bed that semester was an agony (and an ecstasy) of restraint. The first week back we held and kissed, fully clothed. By the end of the second week, we were unabashedly touching each other's breasts — still with clothes. When we at last slipped our hands under the pajama tops (week three), we found such delight that we lingered there a month. By Thanksgiving we were titillating each other with the verbal and even tactile prospect of "touching below the waist" (first with and only then without clothes, of course), and by the middle of December, motivated no doubt by the prospect of a separation at Christmas, we had actually made genital contact and discovered that our bodies not only knew what to do but did it superbly.

We slept very little, grew very thin, and moved around campus in a glow of secret satisfaction. How we managed to contain our joy at the astounding transformations that were overtaking us, I will never know. Not only were we carrying on a clandestine relationship, but our days were exploding with activity. It was as if life's floodgates had been flung wide. We studied less (but better), wrote masterpiece academic papers, engineered complicated and brilliant term projects. Our grades soared, our circle of friends expanded, we joined in more campus activities, and we spent untold hours in song and laughter. Once in a while, just for looks, we went out on a date with a Virginia Man, always returning to each other's arms with a sigh of relief and renewed gratitude for the miracle we were experiencing.

We pretty much pooh-poohed the notion of husbands and decided early on to run away to Samarkand together after graduation. Only occasionally did a shadow suggest to us that even our remarkable love could someday break under the demands of the world. And we were wise enough to know that the joy we had together would be punished if it were discovered. Thus, the cost of our happiness was measured in units of fear and dishonesty, in the little pretenses to friends and the bigger lies to our families.

Sweet Briar's homophobia was hardly unique in the '50s, for nothing existed in the world at large to support same-sex love as a natural expression of affection. Yet Sweet Briar, that women's college of such excellent quality, gave a special spin to society's heterosexual assumption. It called up the best and most blessed of our hearts and minds, and yet it made very clear the fact that we would use that fine education not for ourselves but for our husbands and children — and maybe for a charity or two. As one of my Marxist friends put it later, we were expected to bear and raise the sons and daughters of the ruling class.

Lakey and I stayed together for a year after graduation, getting our master's degrees at an Ohio university. When I entered Illinois's doctoral program, we carried on a long-distance relationship for two years.

Then Lakey got married.

My consummate act of masochism was to be a bridesmaid in her wedding, a classy three-day affair where I felt like the proverbial bull in the china shop — wrong clothes, wrong hairdo, wrong smile, wrong stance, wrong gait, wrong words, and certainly the wrong desires. I knew even as I arrived for the final dress fittings that my motives were not pure. I had wisely decided not to kidnap the bride, but I wanted to see if Lakey really would go through with such a charade. And, frankly, I wanted to rattle her parents, who must have thought she was well rid of me by then.

In a tearful scene in her bedroom the day before the wedding, Lakey admitted that she was marrying to appease her family and that she had been shocked when I agreed to be a bridesmaid.

"You are the air I breathe," she said, "and I know that by doing this, I am cutting off life itself.

But the price of loving you is just too high. I can't hide that way anymore."

I was wild. I ranted and raved, oblivious to her attempts to keep me from being heard in other parts of the house. When none of my pleas reached her, I stormed out of her room and down the stairs, heading I knew not where, but somewhere out of that pain.

At the foot of the staircase, waiting for me, stood a woman I had mentally labeled "Mrs. Amazon." She was the mother of one of the other bridesmaids and herself a good friend of the family's. She was a big woman whose impeccable dress and demeanor nevertheless hinted that she had acquired them only at great psychological cost, perhaps after years of conscious and determined practice. She held out a set of keys.

"Take my car. It's the blue Caddy. And don't come back until you can handle all this."

She put the keys in my hand and very gently touched my shoulder. Then she vanished, back to the solarium, where she was seeing to the proper display of the wedding gifts.

I drove the turnpike at breakneck speeds that afternoon, shouting and sobbing my rage and indignation. It was almost dusk when I came back to the house, subdued, resolute, and still unapprehended by the highway patrol. I made it through the stiff rehearsal without incident and endured the huge dinner seated uncomfortably beside "my" groomsman. I was garbed like a matron in an ill-fitting dress that I had borrowed from Mrs. Amazon. I danced with the requisite number of men of the party, including the groom, made light chatter, and returned the polite enmity of Lakey's parents, until I could escape to the bedroom I shared with other bridesmaids. No further words passed between me and Lakey, nor did I respond to her efforts to catch my eye.

I had decided to leave her to heaven, to get through the formalities and then shake the dust of her world forever from my feet. I wavered only once the following day, when in the ceremony before a packed church, the minister said, "If any man knows any reason why these two should not be united in holy matrimony, let him speak now or forever hold his peace."

In the pause before the minister proceeded, I knew there were at least four people — Lakey, her parents, and Mrs. Amazon — whose hearts were in their throats. I could have made history in that moment. It's to my credit, I suppose, that I declined the opportunity, rationalizing even with no feminist theory to back me up that the word *man* had excluded me from the ranks of potential objectors.

At the reception I dutifully hugged Lakey and wished her well. I made a feeble pretense at reaching for her bouquet when she threw it, musing even as I did so that marriage was already deteriorating the force and accuracy of her passing arm. She and her man took off in a shower of rice, and I went inside to call a taxi.

In the bridesmaids' room I peeled out of the frilly dress and sighed into my rolled-up jeans and penny loafers. I covered myself with my trench coat so as not to offend my hosts and cast a parting look at the reception celebration still in progress in the back of the house. As I waited with my suitcase at the curb, I picked up a few grains of rice and put them in my pocket. The cab pulled up at exactly the same place the happy couple had departed from.

"Greyhound bus depot," I said, putting my bag in the seat beside me.

I never saw Lakey again. In 1980 her husband's letter found me. He said that she had died, the result of a fall and a concussion. He said that she would have wanted me to know.

In the '50s and '60s, my dark closet years, I never felt sick, never felt sinful, and never took my criminal status to be more than the unfortunate result of society's ignorance and bigotry. I credit Lakey with a lot of that self-love, for though our paths had separated, she had clearly been the agent of my greatest self-discovery, and in her hands I had learned my true identity. Thank you, Lakey.

Wood
by
Barbara Wilson

I used to cut wood for her. My parents didn't like
it. "Don't go inside that house," they told me always. But they never said why not.

Trudy had been married or was still, nobody
knew. The house had belonged to a man named
Jim once, then she had come there, and he had
gone. They had kept to themselves, and Trudy still
did. It made her seem unfriendly. It made her seem
strange. It made people talk about her. It wasn't
just that she was single. There were other widows
and divorced women in the neighborhood, and no
one ever said, "Keep away from them."

But I thought Trudy was nice. I was sorry that
everybody was so cold to her. She didn't have
kids, and hardly anyone ever stopped by to see her.
I noticed when cars parked in front and when they
didn't. Mostly they didn't. I'm interested in cars.
For a while there was an Isuzu Trooper, burgundy,
a 1990 model, in Trudy's drive early in the morning three or four times a week. Then it was gone.

I used to wonder if she was lonely. She didn't go
out to work but stayed at home. She told me she
wrote textbooks, that writing textbooks was something you could do anywhere. It seemed like she

enjoyed being at home, working. All the same it was kind of unusual for somebody who wasn't that old. I mean she *was* old, thirty-five or so, but she wasn't ancient.

My family lived two houses down from her and didn't have a lot of money, which is why they let me work for Trudy, mowing her lawn in summer, raking leaves in fall, chopping wood down to size for her wood stove in winter. Trudy could have done all that for herself, but she didn't. She said she was a city girl and had never learned. She said she'd be nervous trying to handle an ax. I was never nervous.

"It's not really work that a girl should be doing," said my father. But my two brothers were younger and lacked the work ethic. It was good for me to have some extra cash.

My mother said, "Just as long as you don't go inside the house." She sounded firm but also pleading. As if she had some idea of how much I wanted to go inside that house, as if she had some idea of the reason why.

It was my mother who put the idea into my head and kept it there.

Maybe if Trudy had been more of an outdoors kind of person, I wouldn't have gotten so curious about her. I would have seen her on the road, walking the dog or getting in and out of her car with groceries or working in her yard. A lot of women in our neighborhood, which is on the outskirts of town and almost rural, are the active type. My type. The type I always want to be.

So I should have disliked the fact that Trudy was so housebound, even on nice days in the summer. But instead, well, it intrigued me. Because I have another side. I'm not a jock; I don't like sports all that much. I like to read, I'm good in English. I've thought maybe I could do something like writing for a newspaper someday. Or even writing books.

In our house we didn't have that many books — I usually got them from the library — but I knew that Trudy had bookcases all through her house. Two big ones in the living room. A smaller one in the bedroom. And in the second bedroom, which she had turned into a study, the walls were lined with books, top to bottom. I had seen all these books through the windows of the house. I saw them when I was raking or mowing or shoveling snow. How beautiful they looked, some old in faded jackets and others bright new paperbacks with titles that promised worlds. Trudy said that some she needed for her textbook writing and some were purely for pleasure. Most of them, in fact. She said she did more research on-line now but that nothing could replace the feel of actual books.

I felt the same. She knew I did. She often loaned me books, handing them through the door, saying, "Tell me what you think of this." Each time I brought home a book from Trudy's, my mother grabbed it and flipped through the pages. I don't know what she was looking for. She was hardly a reader at all. She never had time for it, she said, working all day at Sears and driving an hour there and an hour back every day. But they were only novels, these books that Trudy lent me. Willa Cather was my favorite.

I guess I make it sound like Trudy never left her house, but that's not true. I think she went out during the day, when I was in school. She went to make copies or mail packages or buy more books. Sometimes she went for the whole day to the city two hours away. Sometimes she drove to the city airport and went to another state. She said she had friends there, that it was where she used to live.

My parents thought her life was crazy. "I don't know why she wants to keep living here," said my father. "She must feel that she doesn't fit in, that she doesn't belong."

"It would be different if she worked here, *needed* to be here," said my mother.

"Or if she liked country life…"

"How do you know she doesn't?" I asked them.

"It's peaceful here. It's quiet," said Trudy when I asked her. "I came here because of Jim, and then I stayed. You get used to living outside the city, and it's harder to go back. I get all frazzled when I'm there, see absence everywhere."

Trudy never said what had happened to Jim. I didn't think he was dead, like some people said, people who said they'd seen an ambulance early one morning. Because if he was, he'd be buried in the cemetery nearby, and he wasn't. I had looked.

It was hard at first thinking up reasons why I couldn't go inside Trudy's house. All my excuses sounded lame. Eventually I guess it dawned on her that my parents wouldn't let me. She made a couple of funny remarks about it, but then she stopped. She could see it hurt me. She could see it wasn't my fault. That I would have loved to have come in if I could have.

So instead she came out. Not far. Not into the yard much or as far as the road. She kept close to the house. We talked a lot if she was in the mood. About books, mostly. The ones she read, the ones she wrote. Sometimes she told me about the places she'd been. Who did she see when she went to the city or another state? She never said. I guessed it was Jim. I imagined that they had had a fight, and maybe he had married someone else, and now they were both sorry. I wondered if he had an Isuzu Trooper. I wondered if he had liked to read as much as Trudy and I did.

This went on for about two years, I guess. From the time I was fourteen, in the ninth grade, till the winter of my junior year.

Trudy had been away for quite a while, almost two weeks. The first snows had fallen, then more and more. I had kept her walk clear, waiting for her, and cut up some wood that I'd put by her door.

The day she got back, I was ready. I'd read that last book that she'd given me, *A Thousand Acres,* and I wanted to talk about it. Finally, after school that day, I went by her house and knocked.

When she came to the door, she looked really bad. Not sick exactly but all wasted. Thin, white, tired.

"Did something happen?" I asked.

The cold air rushed between us. I was dressed in a parka and wool pants with a scarf tight under my chin. She was wearing only a robe and slippers, as if she'd been in bed all day. The robe didn't have buttons, and it was velour, like a man's robe, held closed only by a tie around the waist. Something caught at me, below my heart, above my stomach. It was the way the robe opened up over her chest. She had big breasts, swinging free. I'd never noticed that. And a musky sleepy smell.

"Someone died," she said quietly. And paused. "A...good friend of Jim's."

She almost never mentioned Jim. I was pierced. Was she going back to him? Would he come here?

Trudy was shivering in the snowy gusts of wind. "Won't you come in?"

I knew she needed company. I felt so bad. "I want to," I said. But I could see Mom's truck in our driveway, knew I was visible to her, standing at Trudy's door. "I gotta get home," I mumbled. "I just came by to see if you needed any wood chopped, now it's so cold and all."

Wood

"I guess I do," she said as if she didn't care. "Maybe this weekend?"

"Okay!" But just before she closed the door, when I was on my way down the walk, I suddenly called back, "Did you see him? Did you see Jim?"

"Jim?" Her face shattered. "Jim went a long time ago, the first of his friends."

I stood rooted. The snow was falling thick and hard. Her red robe was a slash of color in the white. "Your husband…died?"

"Jim was my brother," she said, so low I hardly heard her, just before the door closed.

I didn't tell my mother this news when she asked, "How's Trudy?" in that critical way she often did. As if she expected to hear something bad.

"All right. Going to chop some wood for her this weekend."

"I thought we might go visit your grandma," Mom said.

"*Mom,* I need the money. Christmas is coming."

"Oh, all right. I'll take the boys. Dad has to work, but he'll be back for dinner. Can you cook him something?"

"Uh-huh." If I knew my dad, the moment he heard Mom would be gone all evening was the moment he'd be joining his friends for a few games of pool. "Don't worry about me, honey," he'd say. "I'll grab a bite at Joe's."

That night around 9, I took the dog out for a walk. The snow had stopped; it was biting cold, the sky was full of stars. I felt at home outside. I had never felt lonely, but tonight I did. As if I wanted someone's warmth close up against me, wanted to feel a heart beating through their skin and mine. I took the usual route, but on the way back I went by Trudy's. I was worried about her.

I came up quiet to the house, but before I got close enough to knock, I saw her in the upstairs bedroom. She was weaving back and forth, red-faced, crying. I didn't know if she was drunk or not. Sometimes when my father got drunk, he went red and weepy. But Trudy seemed more crazy. As if something in her body hurt her and she was trying to get it out by banging around the room and shouting "No!" and "Why, why?"

I should have been scared. I don't know why I wasn't. I wanted to go in and put my arms around her, get her to lie down on the bed, get her to rest. But I couldn't do that either. The dog started pulling at her leash, wanting to go home. I left the memory of Trudy in her room, shouting. I didn't leave the memory of how she looked, naked.

The next day it was snowing again, and by Saturday the world was heavy and white. I thought Mom might not want to drive, but she was determined. "If the roads are bad, we'll just stay the night."

Wood

I waited as long as I could, then I set out for Trudy's. First I shoveled her walk from the street to the porch, then I shoveled a path around the side to the woodpile. The wood had been delivered to her in logs that were too big for her wood stove, most of them. I usually cut them in half and then in half again. I used the ax from home that Dad kept sharp. I liked the clean way the wood fell in two pieces, then two more. It was a good smell, a sweet smell.

All this time I hadn't seen Trudy. When I was finished chopping, I went to her kitchen door and knocked hard. It took a little while for her to come from upstairs. I was relieved to see that she looked like her old self, wearing jeans and a sweatshirt. Relieved and a little disappointed.

"Can I carry some of this wood inside for you?"

"I thought you weren't supposed to…"

"My parents are gone. Besides, I'm gonna be seventeen in three months."

"That old?" she murmured and opened the door wide.

How wonderful it was to be among the books. I saw that her wood stove wasn't even going. She'd been using electric heat. "You should have told me!" I said.

"The heater is just less trouble."

"But the wood stove looks so nice with the flames and all. And it's much cheaper, really, heating with wood."

She smiled at me, and that made me remember a lot of things. I asked if I could wash my hands. She told me the bathroom was upstairs. What I really wanted was to see the rooms there, the bookshelves in the study, and the bedroom.

On the way up the staircase, I noticed some photographs that surprised me. I didn't think a woman like Trudy would have pictures of naked men around. The first one was of a black man with his fly unzipped. Then there was a man out in the woods, tied to a tree. And the third photograph was like a crucifixion or saint picture. A man streaming with blood. All these men had erections.

I didn't look around the way I planned upstairs, and when I came down again, I didn't know what to say.

"Is something wrong?"

"I guess... Those pictures on the wall."

"Oh, God. I forgot about those. I'm sorry. I know they're pretty shocking. They were my brother's. They're by a famous photographer. I don't suppose you've heard of him. He was gay too."

I stared at her. I knew the word *gay*, knew it from afar. Now it was close. I just stared at Trudy.

"Please don't tell your parents. I mean, for my brother's sake. I mean, for mine. He loved living here, but when he moved here, he already had AIDS. Otherwise, he probably would have been out. He believed in that. I don't have an excuse. I should believe in it too. I want to be out, but it's so hard. First I was quiet because of Jim, and then when Lin broke up with me, I mean, how could I come out then?" She was talking faster and faster. "Oh, God," she said, seeing my frozen face. "Now I've done it. Now I'll be run out of town for sure."

All these words all jumbled together. *AIDS*. *Out*. Someone named Lin, the one who had the Trooper probably. In spite of wanting to tell Trudy it was okay, that I wouldn't tell anyone, I found myself walking back out the kitchen toward the door and out the door.

She didn't try to stop me. She had stopped talking and was just standing in some kind of horror. I forgot to ask her for my money, and she forgot to give it to me.

Around 5 Dad called to say he was just going to stop off at Joe's for a beer and a game. "Are you all right, honey? Got enough to eat? Heard anything from your mother?" A few minutes before, Mom had called to say they'd decided to spend the night. The roads had been bad getting to Grandma's; she didn't want to drive at night. Dad sounded surprisingly cheerful about it. "Oh, she definitely shouldn't drive at night. You're all right then? Don't wait up for me if it gets late."

I went into the living room and built up the fire until it was roaring hot. Then I stood near it and opened my shirt as if it were a robe. I touched my breasts, tried to imagine they were bigger than they were, full and ripe and musky-smelling. All those words I had heard this afternoon, I knew them from TV and the news, but now I knew them differently. I knew them from inside. I knew that I had always known them.

When I came outside, it was snowing again — really hard. The wind blew swirls of white into the blackness. All the houses on the street were lit up, and their chimneys puffed smoke. Even Trudy's.

I came up to the house and looked in the windows. I saw her sitting downstairs by the wood stove reading a book. Except she wasn't reading, just staring out in space. When I knocked, she started.

"I just wanted to tell you" I said before she could say anything, "that it's all right. I'm not going to tell anyone. I don't think it's bad. I'm sorry about Jim. I'm sorry about Lin too." That was the end of my prepared speech, and now I stumbled. "Can I come in please?"

She didn't move to let me in. Relief was on her face. "I thought, I thought… It's hard to be brave, isn't it? It's hard to be alone."

I wanted to throw myself into her breasts, to hear her heartbeat, strong and quick. I wanted to be wood and to burn and burn until I was nothing but heat and light in her hands.

She saw my face. She knew. She said, "We're friends then?"

I couldn't speak. I nodded.

Wood

"It's because we're friends that I can't let you in right now. Someday you'll understand that."

She gave me a light touch on the shoulder, and I was outside again. Everything smelled of wood smoke and cold snow.

The Common Price of Passion
by
Jess Wells

"My dearest," Meg's letter said, "someday you will get off the train, and I will take your hand as it hangs by your side, raise it to my lips to kiss the palm that has always only waved good-bye, kiss the hand that has daily held a pen but rarely held me. 'Mine, finally' is what my heart will say. Mine, finally. My lips into your palm, your tiny slip of fingers across my cheeks and nose. Do you know that the mention of a train brings me visions of your wrist and the way I will sleep with the tips of your fingers curled in trust under my chin, your arm in the space between my grateful breasts? Make plans to see me. Tell me you'll be here. It has been too many years of making do with words, and these letters are beginning to show a woman forging hope into desperation. We are the stuff of sex and passion, my darling. That is who we are and must be. Send me faint gesture of a train ticket, a glimmer of a plane reservation. I await your arrival. Be, finally, adventuring."

"My dearest," she wrote later that week, "as I walked through my restaurant, my dress played with my thighs and asked me where you were. Today I dreamt of the down on the nape of your

The Common Price of Passion

neck that leads me to the silk of your hair, of my lips accepting the invitation to bring my tongue to your ear. In my mind your neck has turned to receive my lips a thousand times since I saw you last (two quick days to sustain us for six long months!). Across a thousand miles the shadow of your body presses into mine and tells me that we need to be together, not just in thoughts, in the fleeting moments when the memory of you and the languid sex we shared makes me forget that I am driving in traffic, determinedly foraging for okra worthy of my grandmother's gumbo; not just in midnight visions that are so sweet and tangled that I awake, certain you are bringing strawberries from the next room; not just in the sudden feel of your hands moving up my thighs, trembling with the need to pretend that they do not know where they're going and aren't in a hurry to get there.

"I write, daring to say: Be my lover. Let me see you in the morning wrestling with dreams of bag ladies and your dead father. Let me catch you absently staring out the window, the light warming your skin when you are scowling and you don't notice your beauty, not then nor when you're ironing in your bra or driving. Surely there is a way to capture this passion we have, this desire that makes the paper in these envelopes crackle. Your letters are my bones — they hold me together. They are the strength I need. Your letters arrive, and, mere paper, they manage to be your hands gruffly clasping my face to draw me to your lips, forceful with their passion. How can you dominate me with paper? How can you make me yield, collapsing under the sweet drug of my submission, wanting nothing more than to lie down and receive your skill? I sleep with your letter clutched in my hand, as if it could approximate the warmth of flesh.

"The memory of our fiery times together has kept me alive for years: the rendezvous in midpoint cities, the hotels, the backs of cars, the charade of chance meetings in museums, fleeting, forbidden sex in public places, and then the recollection of those times, the descriptions and dissection. I used to litter my bed with your letters until it was more paper than sheet and rise in the morning singing over the wealth of our love, of the attention and climax each postmark signified. Showering, I was careful of the water, as if each inch of my skin was covered with precious ink that should never be blurred.

"But my dearest, you have to know that something is different now. The fog has brought in a need for comfort. Oh, I know you think that is preposterous, but these are times that require shelter. So I ask you, what is the price of this passion? I look at our letters, and they seem so thin, not infused with the blood and heat of flesh. I am sad. There. I've said it. I ache. If I ask you to meet me, to make more memories, it simply postpones feeling this bruise that I know is there. Did you know

The Common Price of Passion

I had a birthday? That we had an anniversary? I went to a party last week and was the only single woman there and thus subject of pity and cheap sexual jokes. I couldn't tell them about you, couldn't describe what we have. I don't just want you. I want *us*. I can hear what you say: The tension of our separation fuels our passion. Those who know the realities of butter knives and nasal sprays do not know the ecstasy of the flawless passion that we have, you will claim. I can see you pacing through the bedroom, my pubic hairs clinging to unlikely spots on you. You pontificate: 'Consensus is the death of seduction. Would you prefer,' you nearly shout, 'a love scene that begins with the question, "Shall we have sex now or after *Roseanne*?"' Your reasoning and the furious sex you give me later have kept me all these years.

"Is the price of our passion this paper-thin love? All these evenings standing alone in the movie line, taking a book to dinner? Is the distance really what makes the sex burn so bright? You must ask yourself, my darling, which is the fuel — the paper or the love? If it is the love, it would survive. If it is the paper, is it a price worth paying? Write to me, my darling, and as I always close with a plea to see you, I ask you to take me in your arms. Break the mold and come sooner. Plan to be here months early. I cannot wait this time. Feed your wild streak and simply knock down my door. Be, finally, here."

"My dearest," Meg wrote later that month, "you are coming, aren't you? I am standing in such infuriating passivity, as if at an elevator that will not arrive, toast that will not golden-brown. I stomp my foot, and the prep cook puts her head down, chops faster. What can I tell her: I'm anxious for the arrival of the one who makes the sweat slick my body, who cuts my breath into short bursts with a simple move of a hand? I am waiting, and the air crackles with the void. Your letters have stopped since I asked you to fly to me, and I'll say it: I am in pain. The cold air seems to be against my skin all day as if I were not clothed. Where are your words? The memory of your eyes? Even your neck, drinking in the luxury of turning for my lips, moving slowly in a dream every night since, your neck is no longer moving. I feel like an animal lost on a windy night.

"Tell me, my love, can we put this passion away in a drawer like a scarf that doesn't match this morning's suit? And if you would have me do that, then what do I tell the fire in my chest, so willing to send flames into my hands so they will reach out for you, touch you in my dreams, touch me in reply? Shall I pretend I can put out the fire? Stop thinking of your eyes, your smile? Pretend that I could possibly stop the plan to cup the exquisite smallness of your head, the obvious place where these hands were meant to live. You wouldn't ask me to, would you?

The Common Price of Passion

"You are arriving, aren't you? Be, finally, committed."

"My dearest," she wrote in the middle of the night, "I know you're not arriving, and so this will be my last letter. I wanted you to know that there is beauty in the small kiss. It is a kiss given in passing, in public, in airports, before opening the door to my mother's house. It is dry-lipped, close-lipped. It is not gripping or sweaty. There are no flailing arms or tangled legs associated with this kiss. It is tender because it knows the simple pain and fear of everyday life, it knows the unspeakable sounds of early morning. To this tender kiss, laundry is loving. I can hear you shrieking. You consider all these things so pedestrian, but there is, in fact, love and sex in the cups/mops/plates of two lives entwined. Now I wonder, why can't you see this, my beloved? These are not just legs tangled or fingers engrossed in a message but lives entwined. Admittedly, there are no delicious tastes or grateful sighs in picking linoleum, but afterward every step becomes something shared — a thanksgiving — and when every step is a prayer, every object imbued with conviction and appreciation, they each carry their own little moan.

"I have been hearing these moans lately. I thought myself impervious to these sounds but I heard them in a Laundromat, a couple standing in each other's arms watching the tumble cycle, in the theater line when someone offered an umbrella. For the first time I wondered if you would do this for me, and it made me sad. Does our passion actually require so much isolated investment? Why is that we can seem to afford only one type of passion between us? These other lovers have been willing to pay the common price of passion — to watch their sheets grow slightly cold in return for a warm arm clutching an umbrella. Standing in the theater line, the fog dripping off the ends of my hair, I wondered about the price I was paying for the passion we have.

"I saw a couple in their 80s yesterday, and I stopped in the street to cry. They tottered on each other's arms, unable to walk apart any longer, and their clothing was indistinguishable one from the other. Every inch of the two of them had been tended a thousand times by the other. Can you even imagine a passion that could burn not that bright but that long? I need to totter along with someone, my love, to be offered things that are pedestrian like coffee that is just my setting, just my brand, more difficult to offer than lips on my breast.

"My darling explosion of heat, I thank you for the burst of light that you have been, and through the puff of your smoke, I reluctantly give you up. The wider world of juice containers and mortgage payments calls me, offering dry kisses, passionate with a long, quiet history. I say good-bye. Be, finally, alone."

Pasta Salad Made From Curled Noodles

by

Elissa Goldberg

When Delia Minor was ten years old, she learned that in her lifetime she would fall in love three times and three times only. This meant that she had two more love experiences coming, Cousin Edith's dog, Cleopatra, having been number one.

Cousin Edith was Delia's mother's cousin and removed so many times that neither of the women knew quite how they fit together. Edith was older than Delia's mother, Gina, by close to a generation. She was a small woman with a face as wrinkled as wadded paper, and she had three wigs: brunette, pumpkin orange, and frosted. She filed her stubby fingernails as if they were her strongest point, and when she was around Delia, she would tap them on the side table nervously in lieu of conversation.

Cousin Edith's fancy, as she put it, was chocolate cake, and when she visited she would carry a white cardboard box from the Safeway bakery, gooey inside from chocolate frosting rubbed off. She'd hand the box over to Delia as if it were a birthday present. Delia was polite enough to carve herself a large piece and sit in front of Edith as she chewed it, but she always kept her eyes on old Cleopatra, who followed Cousin Edith wherever she went.

Cleopatra was a thick yellow mutt whose joints were as stiff with arthritis as Cousin Edith's face was filled with wrinkles. The two had been together far longer than Delia had known the world. Still, Delia had no compunction about speculating how delicious her life would be when Cleopatra came to her senses and moved in with her and Gina. During each visit, when Delia would turn her cake-sweetened gaze on the dog, Cleopatra would return her look with the same soulful intensity, then move closer to lay her chin over Delia's worn shoes. The old dog would grind her chops, wetting the corners of her mouth, then slowly close her eyes. Some afternoons, when Edith and Gina were absorbed in a particularly interesting piece of gossip, Delia would loosen Cleopatra's head from her feet and lead her slow friend out to the porch, where they'd sit on a dark, cold wooden stair together, Delia's fingers burrowing into the rug of Cleopatra's neck.

On the afternoon that Cousin Edith came to Delia's door with cake box but without dog, Delia's throat closed against any politeness she might have mustered. Even Edith's quivering lips could not quiet the girl's sobs, and Gina finally sent her to her room to wail out her sorrow into her lonesome pillow. It was that evening in her dark,

Pasta Salad

unheated room that Delia understood love. And in a calm made more peaceful by her recent weeping, her life stood before her as if it were a dark landscape set against a light-filled sky, so that the large events clustered into shape. Delia saw that she was to enjoy more love in her future. Blowing her nose, she felt grateful for having known Cleopatra's head on her shoes. When she joined her mother for a late bowl of soup that night, she vowed to herself that she would never again eat chocolate cake.

Delia's parents, Gina Sharpe and William Minor, had married on a Wednesday in July, eleven years earlier, exactly three months after meeting. William had come to hear Gina's piano concert, and though Gina told him and others that it was his eyes that caused her to lose her heart to him, in truth it was his name. Shaking his hand during their introduction, Gina closed her eyes for a moment and envisioned her next round of publicity photographs: "G. Sharpe Minor performing the works of Chopin, Liszt, and Debussy."

Although William had been only William or Will before, Gina took to calling him Bill so that he could stand as a minor third to her G. Sharpe. Needing to complete their triad, Gina became pregnant within weeks and chose a name that started with d — Dean for a boy, Delia for a girl — telling her tone-deaf husband (who was, unfortunately, destined to drown in the river only weeks after his child was born) that their prodigy, in either case, would be referred to as D. Sharpe Minor.

Oblivious to her mother's plans, however, six-month-old Delia took sick. The fever that lasted four days and four nights finally lifted from her limp body, only to take her hearing with it. Delia grew into a child who would appreciate her mother's piano for its smooth keys and ebony finish but never for the plaintive sounds coaxed out of it by Gina's disappointed fingers.

Ever on the lookout for her second true love, Delia tended to annoy the people around her. At the convent school, where she learned to read people's lips, Delia stared at the children in her class. She watched for that particular graciousness in their eyes, that certain brush of their tongue against their lips that would signal, as it had in Cleopatra, unending loyalty and the deepest affection. After the nuns conveyed to Gina the other students' displeasure with Delia's staring, Delia took to watching the children covertly. She began to study their hands and grew to know each member of her class by the size and shape of their fingers: thin and hurried, brown and lined, fat like dough. She watched her classmates from the sides of the playground, prioritizing them on her list of prospective loves by swiftness, the slowest among them being at the very top.

Pasta Salad

Nonetheless, it wasn't until Delia celebrated her sixteenth birthday that she met her next love. Roberto Cisneros, newly arrived from Mexico City, enrolled in her class before he could speak English. Sitting in the desk to Roberto's left, Delia grew fascinated with his dark, slender hands, and when her eyes traveled momentarily up to his face, those hands reached to her desk to shake her startled palm.

From the beginning of their friendship, Roberto allowed Delia to stare at his lips for hours while he spoke words of which she had no comprehension. For him she was the only friend who had unlimited patience with his language skills. Roberto would talk for hours in the tongue that felt the most at home to him, reciting poetry or simply describing his day, while his young friend marveled at his smooth brown trusting lips.

Unlike Cleopatra, however, Roberto laid his head on more than just Delia's feet. And Delia grew to know his lips from more than the silent Spanish that flowed from them. The two of them communicated in words not for their meanings but for the way the words would vibrate between them. Roberto poured Spanish into Delia's navel, murmured it through her hair, and stroked her naked back with its lush phrasing. And Delia would listen not with her broken ears but with her skin and lips and curious fingers.

After nearly half a year, when the two were indeed soul mates, the nuns again called on Gina. This time, however, they included Roberto's mother as well. The meeting took place while the two lovers were walking down what had become their path in a nearby park, their fingers and eyes interlocked, their feet lifting with much effort from the ground, as if their shoes were kissing the earth farewell with each step. It was to be their last walk together. The next day Roberto was removed from school, and the following week Delia learned that he and his family had returned to Mexico City.

Delia took to leaning her broken heart over Gina's piano to feel Chopin's nocturnes rumble against her chest. At night she would wrap herself around her pillow and cry into its folds. In the morning Gina would guide her puffy-eyed daughter through breakfast and push her out the door. But for nearly two weeks, instead of wandering all the way to school, Delia walked her familiar and now solitary path through the nearby park.

On the twelfth day of his absence, Delia received a letter from Roberto written in an incomprehensible language. She folded it into a small square and stuffed it under her mattress. She did the same thing with the next three letters, which were the last. She never heard from him again. But she did keep the four letters her entire life, small yellowed squares filled with cramped Spanish

Pasta Salad

words that were moved from home to home in boxes otherwise packed with her mother's music. And she always knew where to find them.

At twenty-six Delia had grown into, if not a beautiful woman, an eye-catching one. She'd let her dark hair grow to her hips, and because she brushed it only at night and never tied it back, its tangles were constantly falling into people's food carts in the grocery store or getting caught in the car door. Townspeople knew her vehicle by the mane of hair flapping against its roof as it roared past. Delia's nose jutted from her thin face at a sharp angle and was softened only by its freckles. Her eyes were melon green, watery, and almost luminescent. She was a tall woman, with longer than normal arms. Strangers would point her out to others in their crowd. "Look," they'd say. "Did you see that lady?"

She worked then as a bank teller, for although she was not gracious with her customers, the bank officials soon realized that this lip-reader was a genius at math. While she would never make it to loan officer, they intended to retain her as long as they could to cash customer's salary checks and correct their deposit slips.

Delia ate lunch alone. For the first several months of her employment with the bank, she packed a sandwich and spent her lunch break in the staff lounge, nervously flipping through a *Na-*

tional Geographic or *Women's Day* left by another teller. But one Monday, bored with her dreary routine, Delia kept her sandwich in her bag and wandered down the street to Frank's, the Italian deli. At Frank's, Delia discovered pasta salad, and even as she swallowed her first forkful, she knew she would never eat in the staff lounge again.

This was no ordinary pasta salad. It was made from curled noodles that spiraled against one another as if they were sleeping lovers, knees and arms wound snug against backs and thighs. The noodles were in muted colors and cooked just the right amount, light with a satisfying chew. They were dressed with a vinaigrette that left Delia's mouth feeling tingly and aroused. During her first few days of eating at Frank's, the noodles were intermingled with olives, green onions, and boiled carrots. But the salad was always evolving. Some days Delia would find crunchy rounds of toasted almonds or pieces of chicken or the vibrant sheen of a roasted red pepper.

It was during her third full week of eating pasta salad at Frank's that Delia met the pasta-salad maker, Mrs. Manetti. Delia had just put a forkful of cold noodles into her mouth and had raised her paper napkin to her lips when she noticed a pair of hands, the fingers like uncooked sausages, folded and resting on the table across from her. She followed the curves of the stranger's hands to thick arms and shoulders and finally to the double chin, finely lined cheeks, and eyes, soft brown and closely set, of their owner.

"Mrs. Manetti," the stranger said, holding a hand out to Delia.

Delia, who had not had much practice with her voice in her lifetime and knew from her occasional need to speak that people often reacted negatively to her harsh tones, remained silent.

"I noticed how you like my noodles," Mrs. Manetti went on. "You ever want to try something else?"

Delia continued to press her napkin against her lips and shook her head from side to side.

Mrs. Manetti grinned and pushed herself from the table, brushing flour dust from her arms. "Well, I like a woman who can eat," she said. "You come back and visit me anytime." She swung her head in the direction of the kitchen.

After Mrs. Manetti left, Delia's eyes filled with water, but she walked back to the bank with a light heart. Life was delicious.

Every workday after that and several Saturdays, Delia stopped in at Frank's and, after purchasing her plate of pasta, pushed through the kitchen doors so that she could sit on a high stool as Mrs. Manetti cooked. She watched as Mrs. Manetti drained newly boiled potatoes into a colander, the curls of steam rising to mist Mrs. Manetti's glasses and stroke her reddened cheeks. She stared as

Mrs. Manetti deftly sliced a bowl of roasted yellow peppers into strips, their sunlight flesh bursting with juice. Mrs. Manetti would often give Delia small samples of whatever project she was in the midst of and wait for Delia's response. Delia tasted minestrone, apple pastries, sugar-coated walnuts. She tasted new renditions of pasta salad but also, at Mrs. Manetti's urging, other salads: rice salad with peas, marinated vegetable salad, potatoes dressed in a lemon vinaigrette. She often nodded but occasionally frowned. And when she frowned, Mrs. Manetti would frown as well.

"What? Not enough salt? More pepper?"

Margaret Manetti was married to Frank Manetti, a small, nervous man who flitted about the kitchen but usually stood out at the counter, helping customers. They'd been married, Delia learned, for forty-two years, as long as they'd owned the delicatessen. They'd raised three children, who now had children of their own and lived in distant cities. Few of these family details interested Delia. She was content to sit near her aproned friend, who chatted as quickly as her hands moved. And for Margaret, Delia's odd attentiveness, even if she couldn't hear, opened the door on her loneliness and brought in fresh gusts of air.

Frank Manetti's presence rarely worried Delia. She hadn't noticed his shadow in her life's landscape when she'd seen it so clearly at age ten. Delia

Pasta Salad

knew that Mrs. Manetti was hers and was patient to wait until everyone else knew it too. She interacted with Mr. Manetti only to buy her lunch each day. Whether or not her daily presence in his wife's life meant anything to him, he never let on.

One day, only months after Delia's first lunch at Frank's, the doors to the deli were locked. Standing on her tiptoes, trying to peer through the windows, Delia learned about Frank Manetti's sudden and fatal heart attack from a passerby. In a stupor she walked halfway back to the bank, her forehead burning. Then, as if of their own accord, her feet turned around and returned her to the deli. With her heart drumming in her chest, Delia found the moss-covered stairs at the back of the building and carefully climbed them to the Manetti's upstairs home.

She was let in by three young children and watched their large eyes travel up the full length of her tall body. The rooms were filled with strangers, all dressed in black clothes, the women knocking into one another in the tiny kitchen, the men standing at the back of the living room drinking shots of whiskey and occasionally glancing up at those around them.

Delia found Margaret in a chair placed in the center of the room. Margaret's black dress stretched tight across the expanse of her belly. Delia drew a chair alongside Margaret's, and Margaret clasped Delia's hand in her own and did not let go. All day and into the evening, Delia held

Margaret's callused hand as family and neighbors came in and out, offering condolences to Margaret and often to Delia as well.

To Delia, who had known Margaret's hands only by their cleverness in the kitchen, this was a new frontier. She studied Margaret's rough palms with her own soft ones. Her fingers pushed against Margaret's sweaty knuckles and traced the soft flesh at Margaret's wrists. The two women held hands while they ate food brought to them on paper plates by Margaret's daughter. They held hands while Margaret's granddaughter climbed into Delia's lap, leaned against her chest, and fell asleep. They held hands until all of the neighborly well-wishers had returned home, the grandchildren had gone to bed, and Margaret's children sat in weary groupings around them. Then Delia stood up to put on her coat and left for her own home.

Delia returned the next day to hold Margaret's hand through the funeral. Having failed to return from her lunch break the day before, she knew that her tenure at the bank was at an end. During that first week, she stayed with Margaret until her guests dispersed. While the deli remained closed, Delia washed casserole dishes, rearranged furniture, and freshened the flower arrangements.

Three weeks after Mr. Manetti's funeral, Delia arrived to find the delicatessen doors unlocked and Margaret back at her post in the kitchen. She started pulling up a stool, but Margaret shook her head

Pasta Salad

and led her friend to the deli counter. She tied an apron around Delia's waist, pointed to the scale and the cash register, and returned to the kitchen.

After a few months Margaret returned to her chatty self. Customers who were used to Frank's reticence didn't mind Delia's silence. At the end of each business day, while Delia counted money and made notes in the account ledger book, Margaret came to kiss her good night on the cheek. And every evening for the next three years, Delia would smile at her, watch her walk up her back staircase, then turn out the lights and lock the door.

One evening, though, at the end of the three years, just as she had known twenty years earlier, Delia followed her friend up the back staircase after the deli doors were locked. And Margaret, who had been waiting for her, who had even set a place for her at the table, let her in. With water boiling on the stove, the two women sat at the kitchen table and stared at each other in delight, their lips pulled into enormous smiles. They held hands across the waiting plates and then, as if on cue, pulled each other out of their chairs. Delia's hands reached for Margaret's thick waist. Margaret's hands stroked Delia's tangled hair. With cheeks pressed as close as soft noodles, the women danced around the table in the small, steamy kitchen.

The Girl Who Will Become a Dyke and the Boy Who Will Become a Fag Ponder the French Kiss

by
Judy MacLean

Mark climbed in my bedroom window and into my bed. We were sixteen. I kept the light off. We could see each other fine in the glow from the streetlight.

"Did Cinderella enjoy the ball?" he asked.

At last I'd been invited to a prom with one of the acceptable boys the really cool girls dated.

"Yeah," I answered.

"Doesn't *sound* like it was much fun. Was it as good as bodysurfing at Galveston?"

My favorite thing to do in the whole world.

I stretched out on the bed. "Well, no."

"As much fun as Alberto's coffeehouse on folksinging night?"

"Mmm. Depends on who's singing."

"Just as I suspected. Boring as a stuffed armadillo."

"No, Mark, it's just — well, Galveston and folksinging are things I like automatically. Proms are things you have to learn to like. It's part of being mature." I tickled him in the ribs. "Something *you'd* know nothing about."

Ponder the French Kiss

He poked a finger in my own ribs. I laughed, raised a pillow high, and socked him over the head with it. "Oof, no fair!" Mark cried.

"Sh-h, you'll wake up Mom and Daddy," I said, giggling.

We both caught our breath and lay down side by side. We were the same height, five-six, and scrawny. Mark had dark-framed glasses. Until two weeks earlier his wavy black hair had been as long and scruffy as he could get away with and not get expelled. Now it was short. He needed to cut his wind resistance during track season.

"Seriously, Andi, why do you waste your time at a prom?"

"Because I want to be the kind of girl who goes to peace marches *and* gets a National Merit Scholarship *and* reads existentialism *and* goes to the prom." I pushed my frizzy blond hair across my eyes and thrust out my chin. "I vant to taste all uff life," I said in my best throaty foreign-movie-actress voice.

"I'll be honest, it destroyed my supreme respect for you that you even wanted to go," Mark said.

"Every grown-up says high school is the best time of our lives, and this is our only chance to enjoy it," I explained.

In truth I hadn't been able to think of much to say to my date, Brad. The chance that he — or any of the other acceptable boys — would ask me out again was roughly the same as that of an iceberg floating up Buffalo Bayou.

I'd spent most of the night watching Denise Garrison across the table in her low-cut shimmery green dress.

To Mark now I said, "I finally understand why boys like girls with big breasts."

"Some boys."

"I mean, all those pictures of Marilyn Monroe and Brigitte Bardot always look plastic. But Denise Garrison was there—"

"Denise, from trig? With the big nose?"

I elbowed him in the ribs. "That's why you need to go to proms. People look different."

Denise had been aflame with her own beauty. Her soft brown hair, toasted with gold, was pulled back from her face, curling energetically down her neck. The curve of her tanned cheekbones, golden in the candlelight, matched the curve of her breasts below. Vitality sparkled off her. She made little teasing remarks to Chip, her shy boyfriend, who blushed.

Her beauty had warmed me the whole evening. She must think her nose was too big too, but how unimportant that seemed at the prom. I danced in a hazy fantasy of being the one who finally let her know how beautiful and fascinating she was. That little tantalizing smile and those teasing remarks would be turned on me. We'd become friends, there would be slumber parties...

Ponder the French Kiss

"Betty did something weird," Mark said gloomily.

Betty was the school slut. A lot of boys went to her for sex, but she wasn't the kind anyone would take to the prom. Mark had felt daring asking her for a first date on prom night, though he wouldn't set foot at the prom itself. She was pale and sweet-faced, with thick black mascara. Her shoulders were always anxiously scrunched.

I sat up, cross-legged, perpendicular to him, and arranged my blue- and white-striped nightshirt over my knees. "Oh, yeah, I forgot," I said. "How was your date?"

"*2001* was far out. You'll love it. I'd even go see it again with you. And Betty's not like you think. She's *smart*. She's read *Stranger in a Strange Land* too. You should talk to her sometime."

I was silent. In public, at school, only losers talked to Betty.

"You know what your problem is, Andi? You want to be a hippie and Miss Popularity at the same time."

"Well, what's wrong with that? How's that so different from wanting to be a hippie and a track star at the same time? And what did she do that was so weird?"

"We were necking, you know? In the car."

"My, my. Mark necking. That *is* weird."

"Shut up, Andi. Anyway, she put her tongue in my mouth."

"French kissing," I said knowledgeably.

"Yeah. Ever do it?"

"Not really. Well, almost. Maybe."

"She shouldn't have put her tongue in my mouth, should she? I mean, I'm s'posed to do that to her, right?"

I didn't answer. I hated to admit I wasn't sure.

"Think about it, Andi. The boy has the phallus, right?"

We had learned to call it "the phallus" while reading D.H. Lawrence.

"Yeah?"

"And the phallus goes in the girl, right?"

I giggled.

"So I should stick my tongue in her mouth, right? Not the other way around."

"I don't know," I finally had to admit.

"The girl's not supposed to do it to the boy. I'm sure of that." Mark slapped a mosquito that must have entered along with the hot Houston night air when I let him in. He sat up beside me. "Andi, let's try it. That's a way to figure it out."

"French kissing?"

"Yeah."

"Okay."

"First, we try it the way I think is right," he said. We moved closer and stuck out our chins so our mouths would meet. Mark slid his tongue between my lips.

"And-thi?" he mumbled softly.

Ponder the French Kiss

"Mmmph?"

He pulled his tongue back out. "I think you gotta open your teeth," he said, barking an apologetic laugh.

"Sorry, I forgot."

Our mouths joined once more. When I felt his tongue on my lips, I opened my mouth as wide as I would for the dentist. Mark stuck his tongue into the resulting cavern, moved it right, left, up and down, where it gently grazed my own tongue, and I felt slippery wet skin with little bumps. He snapped it back in his mouth.

"Okay, now the other way. You put your tongue in me," he said.

I shot my tongue straight into his mouth the minute our lips touched and did a quick exploration.

"What do you think?" Mark asked.

"Both ways seem pretty much the same to me."

"So you think it's okay that Betty kissed me that way?"

"Probably. Your phallus didn't fall off, did it?"

Mark socked at me with a pillow, but I dodged.

We lay down side by side. The reflections of passing headlights moved across the bedroom ceiling. I smelled his cologne (Canoe) and mine (Miss Dior).

"You know what Coach Gleghorn told us on Friday, Andi? He said, 'I am here to wake up the hero in each of you.' Cool, huh?"

"Oh, here we go again about Coach Gleghorn."

"You gotta admit, he's not your average coach."

"And *you* gotta admit he's human."

"Andi, I couldn't tell anyone this but you. Sometimes, after Gleghorn says stuff like that, I feel a force coming up from the track, pumping my legs faster."

"Let me know when he makes you able to leap tall buildings in a single bound."

"Stop being sarcastic. This is real. The stuff he says goes way over the heads of those guys. Do you think he knows I'm the only one who really gets it?"

Mark was the third slowest on the team, probably no more than an outer blip on Coach Gleghorn's radar screen. But I said, "Sure."

"Do you really think so, Andi? Really?"

"I'm starved. I'm getting some food." I'd been nervous about my date and hadn't eaten dinner. There had been nothing to eat at the prom.

In the kitchen I sliced cold roast beef and rye bread. Then I found some celery and green pepper sticks. I added blue cheese, strawberries, jalapeño olives, tortilla chips, and two big hunks of chocolate cake, piling it on one plate, with two forks. I took a carton of milk and two of my parents' crystal champagne glasses.

Back in the bedroom Mark and I propped pillows against the wall, put the plate between us, and ate avidly.

Ponder the French Kiss

"You know, Andi, there's not too many kids at school who could be on a bed like this together and everything would be okay."

"I know. They're so immature."

I poured milk into the delicate fluted glasses. We clinked them and raised them in toast to each other.

"There might not be two other kids like us in the whole city," he said.

"Or the whole country. Most people think all a boy and girl could do on a bed is fuck."

I turned on my side and propped my chin on my hand so I could look at him. I picked up the last crumbs of chocolate cake with my fingers.

"We might be the first boy and girl to be friends like this in all of history," Mark said.

"Yeah. Back in olden times, girls always had chaperons. They never had a chance to be alone with boys."

"I've never read any books about anyone like us, have you?"

"No, you're right," I said. "We might be the first. But when I grow up, I'm gonna write a story about us. Then the whole world will know."

I yawned big. Food hitting my stomach finally made me sleepy.

"Cinderella's tired. Time to go," said Mark.

"Will you knock off that Cinderella stuff?"

Mark cranked open the window and climbed out. I knelt on the bed and leaned over the sill, the

sweet scent of gardenia rising from the bush outside. I watched him walk across the lawn to his
dad's Ford, thin-shouldered and jaunty in his jeans
and denim work shirt.

Mark and I went away to different colleges. During our sophomore year he wrote me a terse letter
saying he realized he was a homosexual. That
summer in Houston he hung out with a group of
young men and one intense, thin, angry young
woman, who scared me. I felt they were misfits,
contagious misfits, like the kids everyone avoided
in elementary school because they had "cooties."

I didn't see much of Mark until after we both
graduated. By then I had finally met my first
woman lover.

Mark and I reconnected in one of Houston's
first gay liberation groups. One steamy summer
night, about six weeks before the group imploded
from its own conflicts, Betty rode up to the church
basement meeting hall on a big Harley-Davidson.
After the meeting I finally took Mark's suggestion
from six years earlier and talked to her. Turned out
Mark was right. Betty *was* smart. Sweet too.

Becca and the Woman Prince
by
Carolyn Gage

Once upon a time there was a princess named Becca who lived in a kingdom with her father and mother and a great number of subjects, which is why Becca had grown up as an object.

Becca was a curious white girl, and she noticed everything around her. She noticed that the castle floors were always shiny on Tuesday and dull on Monday. She noticed that the cats who roamed the palace halls never came when they were called, which is why no one ever called them. And she noticed that when she played with her marbles, people always told her to do it somewhere else.

Becca asked a lot of questions, but even more than that, she made observations. At dinner she would want to talk about the green beans and whether or not the way you slice them affects the way they taste. At breakfast she would want to talk about the ponies in the meadow and how they toss their heads and why. And at the noon hour she was likely to talk about the dam she built in the creek or the insect larva she had found or the great owl in the oak tree.

But no one ever listened to Becca. Around the palace she was known as Becca the Bore or Becca the Boring or the Princess Who Bores Everyone. And the more people cut her off or got up and left in the middle of a conversation or changed the subject, the more Becca would talk to herself.

Finally the king, in exasperation, decided that the best thing to do would be to marry her off to someone who lived in another kingdom. He sent out announcements that Princess Becca was accepting suitors. And of course he sent out miniature paintings of the princess with these announcements. These, of course, bore little resemblance to Becca, but that was generally the way with these sorts of announcements, and the princes who would respond probably knew that anyway.

And so the first batch of suitors arrived. They were cordial, correct, and uncomfortable. In fact, the best part of their visit was the soccer match they arranged on Saturdays among themselves. Becca came down the second Saturday to play with them, she being very skilled with her feet, but the princes all got uncomfortable again, and pretty soon Becca found herself on an empty field kicking the ball around. The courtship was very structured, and for an hour in the morning and then an hour in the evening, one or another of them would come and talk with Becca in her bower — properly chaperoned, of course.

Well, Becca was charmed to have company that would pay attention to her and not leave for an hour, and she talked almost incessantly. She would occasionally pause for her companion to jump in, but princes are a dull lot, and they couldn't see any point in saying anything since the courtship of a princess has very little to do with whether or not you actually like her.

And pretty soon it was coming to the informal end of the first round of formal suitors. The king waited daily for the expected requests for an audience with him that would indicate that one of them was going to ask for her hand. But the king waited in vain.

The princes had decided among themselves that there was something definitely wrong with Becca. She seemed not to understand her role at all, which at this stage of the game — even before the wedding vows! — was pretty disconcerting. They tried to imagine what it would be like to ride back to their respective kingdoms with Becca talking the whole time or what they would do if she started insisting on joining them in the hunt or for tournaments. Really, she seemed capable of anything. And it was difficult for any of them to feel the sort of manly throb that bodes for a happy marriage when the object of their desire showed not one shred of passivity, helplessness, or submissive behavior.

And so the princes took their leave, each one called suddenly home by some unspecified crisis in the family. Becca dutifully stood on the battlements and waved them off. She was not aware that she had been rejected, because she had never seen herself as up for sale in the first place. The whole thing had been an interesting diversion.

The king sent out a second round of announcements, this time to kingdoms far across the sea, to strange lands where foreign languages were spoken and where the customs and the people were very unlike himself. Because of the unfortunate reports that would inevitably circulate from the first round of suitors, the fact that these countries spoke another language might prove to be an advantage.

These suitors came also, but it seems that Becca's behavior proved disconcerting within the context of many cultures. And the second round of suitors left much as had the first.

The queen at this point stepped in. She hired "tutors" for Becca. She recruited the most fashionable women at court to instruct her daughter about clothing. Becca was fascinated, and she asked so many questions about the point of ribbons and lacings and frills and she had so many questions about why some women wore fancy clothes and why others wore homespun and she made so many commentaries on the effect of fashion on the physiology of the body that the ladies became self-conscious and finally exasperated. They reported to the queen that Becca was mocking them. Becca, as usual, was oblivious to the effect she had on those around her.

Becca and the Woman Prince

The queen hired women skilled in the art of talking to men, which, more accurately put, is the art of listening to men. Becca found the stratagems fascinating, and she enjoyed role-playing the part of the men during the teaching sessions, but when confronted with the real thing, she could never restrain herself from jumping in with corrections or questions about whatever the man had said.

Finally both the king and queen gave up, and Becca was left to her long walks, to her books, paintings, building projects, scientific experiments, and music. And so things went on for a few more years.

And then one day a stranger strode up to the gates of the castle and announced her intention to woo the Princess Becca. A warrior from another culture, she wore a loose-fitting smock over tight trousers, with her bow slung across her back. Around her neck, on a string of bright beads, was one of the battered miniatures sent out by Becca's father. The Woman Prince came bearing a sack of kola nuts to offer to Becca. Her skin was as dark as Becca's was light, and her hair grew out from her scalp in tightly meshed ropes.

The king and queen were flustered. It never occurred to them that a woman would court their daughter. Such a thing had never been done before. Or, perhaps, the queen had a sister somewhere who never married and lived with another spinster, and maybe the king could remember a distant cousin who had a similar arrangement. But surely these were women who couldn't get a husband. Surely they had not *chosen* each other.

The royal pair called in their advisers. The advisers advised them to determine the status of the visitor before they did anything to offend her. Perhaps female marriages were customary in her kingdom...or queendom.

And so they called in the Woman Prince, for such indeed she was. When it was suggested by the chancellor that *Woman Prince* was synonymous with *princess,* the visitor fixed a steely eye on the unfortunate man until his arguments crumbled right out of his mouth. And so the Woman Prince, whose name was Ymoja, was accepted as a prince, and as a prince she had a right, it was determined, to court Becca.

Becca, as was usually the case with things regarding her welfare, was told nothing — only to expect a prince for lunch. Becca was seated in her bower, kicking her soccer ball around under her long skirt and eating the corners off her watercress sandwiches while she waited for her new visitor. She had been experimenting with plant decoctions all morning, and her hands were stained yellow. She had been trying to extract the scent from roses.

The Woman Prince was escorted into the bower by Becca's former governess, who was the chaperon for these occasions. The Woman Prince froze when she caught sight of the princess, who was at that very moment executing a kick that sent the tea table and the sandwiches flying. The governess began to scold her for being so careless, but the Woman Prince trapped the ball between her strong ankles and then gave it a sharp kick, which sent it sailing over Becca's head and through the open window behind her. Becca scrambled over the back of the bench to see where it landed. It just cleared the moat, landing in a pile of rushes on the far side, where it flushed out a pair of disgruntled ducks.

Disguising her admiration, Becca turned to the Woman Prince: "I hope you know you're going to have to go and get it." The Woman Prince turned to the chaperon. The chaperon explained that the Woman Prince did not understand Becca's language. Then Becca, using her hands, explained very graphically how the Woman Prince would need to leave, go down the great staircase, retrieve the ball from the duck nest, and bring it back to her. The Woman Prince stood shaking her head, until finally Becca, completely exasperated, took her by the arm and pulled her toward the door, down the staircase, and out across the castle drawbridge. The chaperon, who had not had her lunch, stayed behind and finished Becca's sandwich.

Becca continued to talk the whole time, which was not unusual, but she did incorporate more gestures into her speech than was her custom. When they reached the far bank of the moat, where the soccer ball lay in the mud, she pointed to the mud and then to the Woman Prince. The Woman Prince nodded gravely, pointing to the mud and then to the princess. This went on for a few minutes, each taking turns pointing and nodding, and finally the princess realized that the Woman Prince was mocking her. Becca had been making a fool of herself by treating the Woman Prince like an idiot just because she didn't speak her language.

Becca smiled at her own stupidity, retrieved the ball, and began to head back to the palace. The Woman Prince stopped her, indicating an interest in some soccer practice. The princess tucked her skirts up into her belt, and the two young women took off. They ran and kicked and rolled until they were both covered with dust and sweat and feeling very good about themselves. Becca smiled at her new friend and said, "I want to learn your language. Teach me."

The Woman Prince understood exactly what Becca was asking, and she said, in her own language, "I will."

And so every day and all day, the Woman Prince and Becca would get together and teach each other their languages. Very soon they could communicate well enough to disagree, and this was a great thing for Becca because no one had ever taken her seriously enough to argue. Their voices would ring out loudly all over the palace, as they ran up the stairs and down the garden paths, talking, shouting, laughing…talking, talking, talking.

Becca and the Woman Prince

The Woman Prince taught Becca about her home, which she called the Bright Country, and how the *jinn,* or spirits, would cause trouble for people if they forgot to carry their *sassa,* a goatskin pouch with magic charms. And the Woman Prince talked about the *simbon,* or hunters, who were protected by two hunter gods, who would become very angry unless their names were always said together because they were so deeply in love with each other.

The Woman Prince spoke of many things, but she never spoke of her family or of the women where she came from.

And the more Becca listened to the Woman Prince, the more she began to notice things — things she had always overlooked even though they had been right in front of her for years. And some of the things she began to notice were boots, especially the boots the guardsmen wore when they were on duty at the palace. One day Becca asked one of the guardsmen where he got his boots. He told her they were issued specially by order of the king. And so Becca went to her father. She wanted a pair of boots. They were better for riding, better for hiking, and a lot better for soccer. She explained how her slippers kept coming off every time she got in a good kick and how this prevented her from following through with a goal. The king sat and listened gravely, nodding his head as if he could sympathize. And so Becca drew out a pattern of her feet for him, gave him a pair of her most comfortable slippers, and gave him a rough sketch of the kind of lacings she wanted the boots to have.

The king sat for a long time looking at the picture of the boots. He continued to look at the picture long after Becca had left. He did not send for a shoemaker. He sent for his wife. And she looked at the pictures of the boots. And then she looked at the king.

They had been willing to allow the Woman Prince to court their daughter. They had even been willing to allow her to marry her and take her away to a foreign country. But they were not willing to let her turn their daughter into a prince. Two princes can't marry, not even two women princes. And who would ever want their daughter after that? It was bad enough that she talked all the time.

The king and the queen realized that they needed to act quickly. Today it was the boots, tomorrow it might be trousers, and who knew after that? Would she want to inherit the kingdom too? It was a bad business, this Woman Prince affair.

The next morning the Woman Prince was summoned to the king's chamber. He had all of his chancellors lined up behind him. The Woman Prince was asked to sit, but she declined. The king, flustered, ordered the chair removed. And then he got down to his point. A mistake had been made. The Princess Becca had apparently been betrothed at birth to a prince from a neighboring kingdom, but because of some remodeling that had been going on in the document room at the time, the record of this arrangement had gotten mislaid, and it had just recently come to light. He, the king, was embarrassed to inform her of this, having granted her permission to court his daughter, and certainly no other prince had ever given his daughter so much pleasure, which only made this meeting twice as painful for him.

The Woman Prince had not moved a muscle since the removal of the chair. She did not look happy, and she did not look sad. She stood like a statue. The king kept coming to the end of sentences and looking expectantly at her. When she didn't move, he would ramble on with another stream of so-of-course-you-sees and believe-me-nothing-would-have-pleased-me-mores. Eventually even the king ran out of stock phrases. Winding down like a toy drummer, he finally folded his hands and sat looking at his chancellors, who made a point of staring in front of themselves, and then he gave up and looked at his lap. There was a long silence. Finally the Woman Prince said something.

Using the king's language, she asked, "Will that be all?"

The king nodded miserably, and the Woman Prince turned sharply and swept a contemptuous gaze across the faces of the chancellors, like a teacher wiping an insult off the chalkboard, and exited. She went directly to Becca.

Becca was astonished. She was puzzling over who this prince could be and how was it that no one had ever mentioned such a thing to her. The Woman Prince finally exploded in her own language: "There is no prince."

Becca looked up, amazed. She spoke in her own language: "What do you mean?"

The Woman Prince for the first and only time in her life looked at Becca with contempt. Becca felt a pain unlike anything she had ever experienced. And in that instant she knew that she would leave her castle, leave her people, leave her language, leave her innocence about the world — that she would leave everything she had ever known and learn another whole way of living in order that this woman whom she loved with all her heart and all her soul and all her body would never, never in her life, ever, have a reason to look at her that way again. And she knew that the price could be nothing less.

Becca rose. "I understand," she said in the language of the Woman Prince. "I will leave this place. I will leave tonight."

The Woman Prince looked at her. Becca was standing, but she was not as tall as the Woman Prince, and she needed to tilt her head in order to look in her eyes. Becca repeated, "I will leave this place. Tonight."

Becca and the Woman Prince

The Woman Prince, in a palace of lies, in a palace of liars, looked long and hard into Becca's eyes. "I won't take you," she said.

Becca, stung for a second time by her lover — but this time by her words — answered her.

"I didn't ask you to. I am leaving because I don't belong here." She turned to leave, but something didn't seem right. She turned back to the Woman Prince and took off her ring. She held it out to her. "I want to give this to you because I love you."

The Woman Prince looked at the ring, an expensive ring, a white woman's ring, the ring of a princess. And then she looked at Becca. Becca nodded and put the ring back on her finger. Great tears began to roll down her cheeks. The Woman Prince knew they were not for her. She knew they were the tears of a white girl who for once could not have what she wanted. And she turned and left before the tears rolled down her own cheeks, tears for an African Woman Prince who was so brave, so very alone in a palace of liars.

And that night the queen drank more wine than she had in years — maybe as much wine as she had the night she and her girlfriend had gotten drunk and spent the night together almost forty years ago. The king took a potion, because he didn't like the night.

Becca stuffed the cracks around her door and her windows so that the light wouldn't shine through, and she packed. She packed carefully, for the first time in her life having to worry about survival. In a way her great heartache made the task easier. What could she fear when she had already lost the greatest thing in her life?

The Woman Prince paced the battlements, which were outside the large window of her chamber. She had come here — why? She had seen a picture of the white princess. Why had she come? Because in her kingdom they had no use for Woman Princes. Because her brothers were the ones who would inherit the kingdom. Because where she came from, the women would be given in marriage to the men. Because this was a chance to go somewhere different, to start all over. What had she been thinking? And if she had married Becca, where did she think she would take her? Home again, where Becca would see that she was only a princess in her own kingdom and not a Woman Prince at all? Wasn't this the ending she had known would have to happen all along? Stupid, stupid woman. Stupid. And part of her heart was hard for the soft white girl who had been content to be a princess. And part of her heart cried out for that girl, because they had laughed and wrestled and argued and played soccer.

And the great and proud Woman Prince paced until the light of dawn began to appear in the sky. And then she heard the sound of the drawbridge being lowered, slowly — oh, so slowly. And with a shock she saw Becca — Becca in boots — leading her little speckled pony across the drawbridge. And then she saw her throw a bundle up on the saddle and swing herself onto the back of the pony. Becca, who didn't even know how to build a fire. Becca, who had no idea what the world was like. Becca, her lover, was riding out alone across the misty fields.

And in an instant, a blind and rushing instant, the Woman Prince tore back into her room, grabbed her bow and her sassa, and dashed down the great stairway, past the castle, and into the courtyard. She ran past the sleeping castle guards, past the dazed gatekeeper with his stocking feet and his shiny new gold piece. The drawbridge was still down, and racing over it, the Woman Prince could just see Becca on her pony in the distance. She lifted her voice and called out with her fiercest warrior cry, a cry that pierced the fog and rang across the damp fields as she broke into the long, even strides that had carried her so many miles from her African homeland — strides that carried her now into the red glow of the now-risen sun.

In the morning the king and the queen were not surprised that the Woman Prince was gone. That she had left her belongings seemed odd, but no one really wanted to talk about the episode, and the queen ordered the things to be discreetly packed into a chest and labeled and carried down to the cellar — in case the Woman Prince should send for them. After all, this was as much a question of diplomacy as hospitality.

There was a note on the princess's door that she did not want to see anybody or talk to anybody. And, frankly, nobody wanted to see her or talk to her — and so the note, the door, and the princess were left undisturbed.

It was not until the second day, when the servants began to whisper about whether or not the princess was eating, that the queen felt compelled to knock on her door. Too embarrassed to admit that her daughter would not speak to her, she reported that Becca had a sick headache and wished to be left alone.

As usual it was the working women who figured out what was really going on. No food, no water, and especially no chamber pots to be emptied — either the princess was killing herself or she was not there.

On the third day one of the maids took it upon herself to climb out on the ledge of the castle wall and peer into the window of Becca's bedroom. The room looked as if a whirlwind had torn through it. Chests were open with all their contents spilling out, clothing was strewn all over the bed, and the bed itself was torn apart — but no princess.

The queen became hysterical. The Woman Prince had kidnapped her daughter and was holding her for ransom! The king made unfortunate remarks about foreigners in general and women princes in particular. But, as always, it was the working women who figured out the truth. They noted that the mayhem in Becca's room was not indicative of a bloody struggle but of a hasty flight. The ransacking, chaotic as it appeared, actually represented a thorough but hurried search for items whose existence, value, and whereabouts could have been known to only their owner. Besides, anyone who had ever seen the two women playing together would have known how utterly unthinkable it was that either one of them should dominate the other for a minute longer than might be absolutely necessary to kick a field goal.

And so the queen, who had made a fool of herself by reporting the conversation with Becca, retreated to her bedchamber — and her wine — with her own sick headache. And the king, with some embarrassment, ordered destroyed the posters announcing a reward for the capture of the Woman Prince. A great silence descended on the castle. Becca's things were bundled together into several chests, labeled, and sent to the cellar also. And the queen ordered a lock be placed on the door to Becca's room.

The chancellors, the king, and the queen never made mention again of either Becca or the Woman Prince, and the servants learned to follow their example — at least when they were not among themselves.

As the years went by, rumors began to reach the palace of two girl knights — one black and one white — who were riding about the neighboring kingdoms punishing acts of violence against women and teaching girls to defend themselves. There were some who swore the whole thing was a myth, and there were others who believed in the knights but who insisted they were two young men. And there were others — young girls of a marriageable age, mostly — who just disappeared one night and were never seen again by their families.

And years and years later, after wars and famines and plagues had ravaged the kingdom of Becca's childhood, a rumor reached the ears of the aging king. The queen, alas, had died many years earlier from an unfortunate fall from her bedchamber window.

The rumor was this:

That at the very remotest corner at the far ends of the earth stood a small cottage and a lovely garden with a creek running through it. And in this cottage lived two older women — one black and the other white — who had many visitors from near and far but always women. And these visitors would come away struck by how much the two women loved their garden and how much they loved their animals and how much they loved their charming home, but the thing that would impress the visitors most was how much the two women loved — absolutely loved — talking to each other.

If This Were...

by

Antonia Matthew

We're leaving the bookstore after going over finances. It's late. We have to go out by the back door into a dark alley. You go down the rough wooden steps first. There's no handrail. I lock the door, shake the knob to make sure, and start down. You're waiting for me. Where the steps are no longer protected by the roof and the rain catches on them, there's ice. I slip and start to fall. You reach out.

"Thanks," I say. "Everyone manages to avoid that icy patch except me."

You laugh. "Now, if this were a romance story, you would find yourself melting into my embrace, and our lips would meet — instead of you apologizing!"

I'm caught off-guard by your remark, coming from such a businesslike woman, the store's bookkeeper for five years.

"I guess that's right," I say slowly, "and then warning alarms would go off in my head; I would pull away and rush across the alley to my bike."

"Oh, yes," you respond, "and unlock it — fingers fumbling — climb on, and as you ride away I'd call, 'Are you all right?'"

"And I'd shout back, 'Yes, I'm *all right,*' and disappear down the street confused and shaking."

"While I'm left behind, staring after you, angry with myself."

Still laughing, we cross the alley, and you wait while I unlock my bike; then I wheel it over with you to your car. You climb in and wave as you drive off.

I get home, feed the cats, stare into the refrigerator, wondering about supper. The phone rings. I stumble over a cat and manage to pick up the receiver before the machine starts up.

"Yes?"

"If the phone rings, you're supposed to let the machine answer, sure that it's me calling. You stand and listen to my voice, feeling confused all over again," you announce firmly.

"Oh, yes, of course," I say, surprised, laughing, "and...uh...before you pick up the phone, you've...uh...poured yourself two fingers of scotch and put Vivaldi on the CD player, telling yourself you do nothing right," I finish in a burst.

"But if you do answer the phone, I say your name, and you say, 'Yes,' and then there's a significant pause. Then I say, 'About just now...'"

"And I say, 'There's nothing to say about just now.' Then *you* reply, 'If that's how you want to handle it.'"

"And you answer, 'Yes, that's how I want to handle it!' then slam down the phone."

If This Were...

"After doing that, I wander disconsolately around the house, picking things up and laying them down."

"And I," you say, sounding breathless, "I stand holding the phone, staring out of the window into the shadows of the pines, before setting the receiver slowly down; and after two more belts of scotch I go to bed reminding myself that I'm not going to get involved again. Nothing happened."

"And finally I go to bed, pushing out of my mind the feel of your arms around me, the brush of your lips on mine, the excitement in my body."

We laugh, say, "Good night," and hang up.

The next evening as I'm locking up the store, you come in, your arms full of assorted bags as usual. You have the completed accounts and make sure that I understand what you've done. I thank you and file them.

"Now what?" you say. "Do you want to play some more?"

"Well, all right," I reply.

You smile and set down your bags. "So the next day I come by. I talk about practical things, go over the accounts with you — just like we did! But then I say, 'Are you *sure* everything's all right?'"

I grin. "I say, 'Yes, of course I'm sure. Why shouldn't I be?' and I start to lock up."

"Okay!" you say, getting into this. "I can't believe that you're shrugging me off, but all I say is,

'Gotta go,' and leave. But the next day yellow roses are delivered to the store, and you arrange them in a vase on your desk."

This surprises me, and I begin slowly, "As I take them out of the paper…I look in vain for a card, uh…my heart beats faster, and I start to sweat. I say to myself, *Who else but she could have sent them?* and I feel out of control. I both want and don't want to see you. How's that?"

"You're doing great," you say. "Okay — I don't come by the store that day, and you're disappointed."

"I put the disappointment out of my mind and go home, feeling slightly dissatisfied with my loved and familiar surroundings." I stop. "I'm losing the story line," I say. "So if you don't come by, where are you now? Are you going to get involved in a new project to put me out of your mind?"

You consider this. "Perhaps, or decide that I have to see you again."

"Let's go with that. Possibly, you stop off at my house a few evenings later on some pretext — more papers to be signed. And although I've begun to decide that there really *was* nothing going on and feel annoyed, I invite you in and offer you coffee. As I start the old percolator, I'm wondering whether to say anything about the flowers. You come into the kitchen, and we look at the papers. You stand very close to me, and I'm not sure whether to move away or not."

If This Were...

"I reach across you to point out a figure, and my hand brushes your breast. You gasp and step back, color rising in your face, your breath coming in quick gasps."

"I say, 'The coffee's ready,' turning away, trying to regain control."

"But I follow you, touch your shoulder, say, 'I really need to talk about Monday.'"

"I tell myself that I have to be firm. I have to say no. And I pour the coffee, hand you a mug."

"But I set it down, look deeply into your eyes, say, 'You felt something when I held you, when our lips touched.'"

"I'm silent, confused. I want to lie, to say, 'There was nothing. I was shocked after falling. I didn't know what I was doing.'"

You interrupt me. "But instead you say softly, 'I felt something. But I didn't want to. I don't understand myself.' Then I say, 'I'm very attracted to you.'"

"But I've got to gain some control," I say. "So now I'm going to interrupt at this point. I'll say, 'I don't want to hear this.'"

"But I ignore you and say, 'I knew you felt something. It wasn't just me.'"

"And I reply slowly, 'Yes…but…it's never happened before… I didn't ever imagine…and with you.'"

"Then I can't restrain myself. It all comes pouring out, 'I want to hold you. I want to kiss you.' I move nearer and put my hands on your shoulders. Your breathing is coming really fast now…"

"And alarm bells are going off like crazy, but I'm drawn inevitably toward you."

"I reach out to touch your cheek, your hair."

"I move closer toward you, drawn by your lips. Your arms are around me; you bend to kiss me."

"I slide my hand into your hair, hold you, press my lips to yours, and gently with my tongue push into the warm, welcoming wetness of your mouth."

"I gasp, I go weak at the knees and moan as your hand slides down my back, holds me firmly to you…" Then I stop. "Whoa!" I say. "We're moving pretty fast here. I think we need some more alarm bells — the door or the phone. We can't let it all happen right now; we're not far enough into the book. And anyway, don't we need an ex-lover or some reason that makes this whole behavior inappropriate, unprofessional?"

"Uh, yes, I suppose so," you reply, "but it was getting to be such fun."

"But it's all happening too quickly and too soon. We need some sharp rejoinders. We need a drawing back, like days or weeks when we don't see each other and we can't concentrate and our lives are falling apart."

"Oh, yes!" you say, getting into this new approach. "How about a lack of trust or an expectation of betrayal brought on by some never-forgotten early trauma?"

If This Were...

"Goddess!" I exclaim. "How do we fit all this in? This stuff is much more difficult to make up than I had thought."

"Okay, maybe we need to include a friend to admonish one of us after we have confided in her, the friend. See, one of us is straight — well, sort of. Confused, anyway. Perhaps is engaged to some suitable guy. Doesn't have her shit together."

"No! You can't say that in this genre."

"Well, her act together then."

"All right," I agree. "What about putting in something to separate them — like one has a foreign assignment or is taking a sabbatical?"

"Or has an accident, and the other one doesn't know about it."

"But that only happens in het stories."

"Not so," you say. "What about when the boom fell on Alex?"

"Yeah, but Lee was there when it happened — heck, she *did* it!"

But you don't give up. "What about Jennifer? She was scarred on the battlefield and hid from Maggie."

"Yeah!" I say, getting excited, "and Maggie *found* her!"

"That's right! See, I *told* you that we could have an accident."

"Hmm, all right," I say. "But there are other things, you know, like a misunderstanding about a relationship with a friend."

"*And,*" you say, "several obligatory scenes... like in the shower." Seeing my expression, you add, "But not right away."

"That's right. We have to have the two-steps-forward, one-step-back sort of thing. One initiating something and then pulling away and both pretending that nothing is really happening."

"We mustn't forget the driving scene. You know, slim, strong hands on the wheel, competent handling of the car, fine profile..."

"And beautiful clothes that enhance the color of the eyes, scent that lingers in the memory, apartments with carefully chosen treasures...and cats," I add. "We have to have cats."

"Listen," you say, "this is getting complicated. We have to start taking notes. How about if we go back to my place and start writing this down? And incidentally, do you have a vase?"

And you pull out of one of your bags a bouquet of yellow roses.

Swing Shift

by
Julia Willis

I was on the swing shift then. And when I got off over there at Merita Bakery that night, what I thought was, I'd go pick up Rochelle, who was waiting on me, see, and we'd go down to the Scorpio for a drink and a dance. It not being no later than 11 o'clock. Specially since on Saturday nights the Scorpio just begins to get interesting around midnight. Now that was my plan. But Rochelle, she had a little plan of her own.

I let myself in with the key she kept under the empty flowerpot. The hanging light over the kitchen table was on, but the rest of the house was dark. You'd of thought nobody was home, except for her Honda was in the driveway and the radio was on real soft in the bedroom.

I followed that music on back through the house, my body kinda tingling, you know, like it's gonna be touched real soon. Her bedroom door was open just a crack, and I pushed on it till I could see Rochelle's water bed by the light of one of the fat orange candles she had made a bunch of in Maxwell House coffee cans. I didn't see her, though. I just heard her, giggling behind the door. So I pretended like I didn't hear a thing and walked on into the room, giving her a chance to sneak up on me good. Which she did and tackled me right onto the bed and jerked off my baggy white work pants dusted with powdered sugar. And honey, she loved me so good, I didn't know which way was up. It was funny too 'cause just coming from being on the line for eight hours, I could close my eyes and still see those mini doughnuts coming down the belt and my hands reaching for them — two at a time, two at a time.

And is this crazy or what? I don't know why, unless it was the doughnut holes, but having that in my head made me so damn excited till I must've come five times before she let me catch my breath. And you know what was playing on the radio? That real old Nat King Cole song "Unforgettable." Just him singing by himself. This was way before his girl Natalie went and had it fixed to where they could sing together even though he was dead. Which is a good thing. I don't believe I could've come five times to any song a woman was singing with her dear departed daddy, know what I mean? Kinda creepy.

Anyway, that Rochelle, boy, she was a hot one. And this was not no one-way thing neither. When I loved her back, she just carried on, first calling my name and then the Lord's, bucking that water bed like a dolphin in heat. I could've stood her leaving the Lord out of it, but I loved the way she said my name, like "Oh-Becky," like it was all one word, in that voice of hers that seemed to crawl up out of her throat like a rock scraping sandpaper. It gave me the shivers every time she said it, which naturally spurred me on to greater and greater heights of pure passion.

Damn. I tell you, it was a real shame about me and Rochelle, how that didn't last, how it couldn't get past her drinking and me being on the swing shift, because in the lovemaking department it stayed so good, I believe it would've stayed that way forever.

But I'm getting off the track here. I just had to explain how we ended up in bed instead of out at the Scorpio that night.

And we stayed there a pretty good while too, doing one thing and another till somebody, long about when the bars let out and we were past that point where love is all you need — and it was probably me 'cause I hadn't had no dinner — said, hey, let's get up for a while and go get us something to eat. So we fooled around a little bit more, and then we got up. I didn't even shower or nothing, just pulled my work clothes back on and went out into that warm spring night feeling like it was all mine and like Rochelle and me had to be the most fantastic women in the whole world. But also kinda feeling like everything was so intense that if a gnat landed on my arm wrong, I'd have another screaming orgasm right there in her front yard, standing up. So I handed her the keys to my Chevy

Malibu. "Here," I said, "you better drive, honey. I got to pull myself together."

"You need to eat," she said.

We knew without saying where we were going. After 2 in the morning on that side of town, when the queer bars let out, you either went to the IHOP off the interstate or the White Tower on East Boulevard. That was it, that was the selection, A or B, take your pick. Anyplace else that time of night, and it could be you'd find trouble, and why go looking for it? Now, if we had been to the Scorpio, Rochelle would've driven us on over to the IHOP, but from her house the White Tower was closer. And we got there just in time too. Ten minutes later, and we couldn't have found a seat, much less a booth.

The White Tower was like somebody took a square made of brick on the back and glass on the front, stuck a grill and a horseshoe counter with booths along the sides in it, slapped on a flat tar roof, and plopped it down in a parking lot across from Friendly Auto Parts. It was not near as fancy as the IHOP, in other words, so you can just imagine. But the food was still good as anything you get that time of night, and the service was a whole lot better. As long as I went there, which had to be five or six years, right up till they closed it, I never knew but two night waitresses to work there steady. It was always Hazel and Cora. You might see somebody else filling in but never regular.

Swing Shift

Hazel and Cora and a long string of come-and-go short-order cooks who traveled the White Tower circuit between binges.

Cora was the quiet one, the one with the sunken cheeks and the hair net, the one who would look exactly like your grandma if your grandma was destined to spend her golden years on the graveyard shift at the White Tower, standing on her feet for eight straight hours and chain-smoking Marlboros in a white china saucer by the cash register. But it was Hazel who really ran the show, almost like the White Tower was her house and whoever came in was visiting. Not that she overdid it. She might tell you how her son was getting along in Las Vegas and how if she was to go out there, he promised to take her to see Elvis — now that tells you how long ago all this was. And if you were any kind of a regular, she'd know how you liked your eggs or your burger or how you took your coffee or what kind of pie was your favorite, but she did it real low-key, back and forth, waiting on you, checking on you, without ever intruding on your privacy, not the least little bit. It was a real gift. Hazel was one of the most restful people I ever met, and yet you knew underneath all that easy charm there was a steely little woman who could spit nails in your eyes if you crossed her. And I love a woman who's got her limits, don't you?

Well, this particular night Rochelle and I got a booth on Hazel's side, but she was busy at the register, so Cora took our orders. I don't remember what Rochelle had, but I know I had a burger and fries because I hadn't been out drinking. I never had breakfast there unless I was pretty drunk. And I might've been tired and hungry and walking on legs like Jell-O from making so much love, but I was sober as a damn judge. I'm sure I was about the soberest customer Hazel and Cora were gonna see that night. Even Rochelle had been having a few beers waiting on me to get off work. So maybe that's why I felt like I paid more attention to what was going on, being more sober and less driven by my lust, at least till I got done eating, than the rest of the crowd. But maybe not.

Like I say, we had our food ordered before the place filled up, but it did fill up quick, with one or two familiar faces from the Scorpio but mostly with people from Oleen's, which was the smaller and older and not-so-trendy bar. Meaning it was the neighborhood bar for the queens and the fag hags and this one bartending dyke who did a pretty fair Wayne Newton imitation. Plain old androgyny was a little unsettling for Oleen's, so neither Rochelle nor me went there much. Rochelle waved at a couple of Oleen's guys when they came in, but I was not in a table-hopping mood, still being in my work clothes and reeking of sugar and sex.

"Would you mind if we sat with you?"

This came not from one of the guys Rochelle had waved at but from a boy we didn't know, a boy in jeans and a feed-store cap who looked fresh off the farm and had a dark, sultry drag queen in purple satin beside him.

"No, not at all," Rochelle said, leaping at the opportunity to come sit with me. I'm telling you, that girl could not get enough. She squeezed up against me like there was no room and whispered, "You smell like a cookie that's just been laid."

This couple sat down across from us, and the boy took off his cap and spoke first. "My name's Joe," he said.

"Lila," the drag queen said, adjusting her black evening gloves.

Rochelle asked Joe where he was from, and he told us about this horse farm out in the country he was trying to make a go of. I asked Lila where she was from, and she said Hollywood. Naturally.

"Isn't she beautiful?" Joe was really taken by her, just in awe, and you could see why — there was something so horselike about Lila. I mean that as a compliment.

"Are you a nurse?" Lila asked me. 'Cause I was dressed in white, I guess. It was real sweet the way she asked me too, like she was being polite and sincere at the same time.

Rochelle laughed and leaned on my shoulder. "She works in a bakery."

"Well," said Lila, like she had practiced for this moment, "nothin' says lovin' like somethin' from the oven."

See what I mean about sweet? I never met a real woman, myself included, who was ever that sweet. That's the real beauty of drag queens, how they always strive for perfection.

Hazel brought Rochelle and me our plates and set them down with an eye on Lila and Joe. "Y'all just got here, didn't you?" She didn't miss a trick. "Do you know what you want?"

Lila put a gloved finger to her chin. "May I see a menu, please?"

"You surely may," and Hazel handed her one from its holder behind the salt and pepper.

Lila took that menu like it was an invitation to a fancy dress ball, gave a loving glance to Joe, and announced to the rest of us, "We'll share." I thought Joe would melt into a little puddle right there in his seat. Oh, he was a happy man.

So Hazel, wanting to give them a minute to decide, said "I'll be back" and went to ring up somebody else's bill.

Lila barely scanned the menu before she presented it to Joe. "Everything's good," she purred.

"I bet it is, baby," he grinned. And you knew they weren't talking about the food at all.

Then Lila turned her attention to me again. "Are you sure you're not a nurse?"

Rochelle stroked my arm and said, "She may not be trained, but she has got the healing touch."

"Ooh," Lila said. And you knew they weren't talking about nursing at all.

Swing Shift

It was right around then the trouble started. There was this old Buick with a hole in its muffler, lights on and the engine running, pulled up right out front. There was this big kid, a teenager who'd taught himself to walk like a gorilla, leaning on the driver's door and talking to some other kids inside. You remember these things later, when at the time it doesn't mean anything. I probably wouldn't even have noticed except I was too busy eating to do anything else but look around, see who was there, wonder if that Ford pickup loaded with bales of hay and facing Friendly Auto Parts was Joe's, and try to picture Lila sitting up there in the back on the hay like a beauty queen on a parade float, smiling and waving. That was a pleasant thought, and I like pleasant thoughts when I got my mouth full.

Maybe Rochelle asked me how my burger was, or maybe I looked down to pick up a french fry, but next thing I knew that teenage ape-man was over by the register with Hazel. From the way he was so jumpy, huffing and puffing like he just ran in a touchdown, it didn't seem like he'd come to order take-out. For one second it crossed my mind he was about to rob the place, and it might have crossed Hazel's too, 'cause when he got her attention, she sized him up good with a look. But he had no weapon except his mouth, which he proceeded to shoot off real quick and real loud.

"Do you know," he shouted, "this place is full of nothing but queers?"

Julia Willis

Now Hazel didn't say so, but for him to be assuming there was no straight people at all in the White Tower — that was not quite how it was. True, most of the straight crowd had cleared out temporarily, but there was at least one booth where you could tell the two dating couples who hadn't got their food yet were straight by the way they were keeping so still, hoping to blend into the Formica. Then along the counter up front there was probably four or five guys from the neighborhood — which was a nice ethnic blend of rednecks, hippies, and Lumbee Indians — and those boys had to be either too drunk to notice the queers or didn't give a shit in the first place. So the White Tower was not full of nothing but queers, and that turned out to be a mighty important distinction later on. But we're not there yet.

Well, the room got real quiet, just like on a TV Western when the bad guy comes in through those swinging doors and the poker game stops and the piano player quits playing the song about the buffalo gals or whatever. Like you could feel everybody — all the queers, anyway — giving off this one big sigh like, "Oh, no, not this shit again."

First thing Hazel did, now she knew what he was up to, was give him one of those grins that goes, "Yeah, so?" Then she said something I didn't catch. Whatever it was, it made him madder.

"You mean you're not gonna call the police?" he sputtered. You talk about angry? That boy's ugly face was all red and blotchy, and I mean you could almost see little flecks of foam on his lips, he was that pissed.

There was about two seconds of dead silence before Hazel gave a little cackle, turned her back on him, and walked away. Now that threw him. He stood there, fuming, blinking his eyes like somebody had just pulled off his rock and shined a flashlight on him, for about two more seconds of that same dead silence, and then he was out the door, whacking it so hard with both arms, it's a wonder it didn't crack the glass.

That Buick with the bad muffler gunned its rumbling engine when he jumped in the backseat, and they peeled out across the parking lot making this high-pitched squeal, what you'd call the automotive equivalent of a whole carload of assholes pumping their armpits to get attention.

Then an older drag queen sitting at the counter with her makeup on crooked and one spaghetti strap falling off her shoulder broke the silence by folding her hands, rolling her eyes toward the ceiling, and screaming, "How rude!"

That did it. Everybody laughed, even the uptight straight couples, and everything in the White Tower took on this rosy kinda glow where everybody's looking around and thinking, *Here we are, and it's okay now,* like when the plane hits a pocket of turbulence and after it's over everybody's so relieved, not only 'cause it's over but 'cause it probably won't happen again. Not on that flight, anyhow. We always like to think things like turbulence, lightning, and queer bashing never strike twice in the same spot in the same night. This is not true, this is all nonsense, but if you didn't play tricks on your mind sometimes, you'd go crazy every damn day.

Lila was the first one at our table to say anything. "Well," she said, "*somebody* didn't get his nooky tonight."

Joe sat up a little straighter in his seat. "Yeah, but he's gonna get something else if he's not careful." He clenched one fist and rested it on the table beside the silverware rolled up in his paper napkin. You could tell Lila appreciated his gesture by the way she placed her gloved hand on the elbow of his denim jacket.

"Y'all decide on what you want?" Hazel had returned, with the look of the pilot who got us through the turbulence and now expected the rest of the flight to be uneventful. Or was pretending she did, at least.

"Hazel, what did you say to that guy?" I just had to ask.

"Oh, him," she said, like it was already a boring memory. "Told me they was queers in here — I says, 'Well, that ain't no skin off your nose, is it?'"

"Right on, sister," said Lila.

"Well," Hazel went on, "I think it's stupid. I can't see what it is makes 'em so mad — if they don't like it, they don't have to do it. Now what'll y'all have?"

Lila ordered the most exotic thing she could find on the menu — cinnamon French toast. Joe wanted plain old steak and eggs. And Rochelle wanted to go home. She had got awful quiet, not eating much, just playing with her scrambled eggs, piling one forkful on top of another.

"Let's get out of here," she said. "I can't stand that kinda stuff." Rochelle hated yelling and violence 'cause she grew up with so much of it. Once she got stirred up, it was hard to convince her the turbulence was over. But I had to try.

"Okay, I'm almost through." When really I was counting on a piece of lemon meringue pie. I mean, I had picked out the piece I wanted in the dessert display and everything, so I was wanting to talk her into it. "Don't you want a piece of pie? Split one with me?"

"Uh-uh."

I put my arm around her. "It's okay, honey, really it is."

Now I had no more than got those words out of my mouth when all hell broke loose. I don't know where he came from, that same red-faced angry Mr. Teen Asshole — I didn't see the car or his friends or nothing — but there he was again, in the front door, up to the counter, and picking on this poor guy who just happened to be on the first stool he came to. He wasn't yelling this time, it was

more under his breath, "Faggot, you wanta fight
me, you damn faggot?"

I swear, the way those same fool words come
out of their mouths, you'd think they took a fuck-
ing course in nasty, only they're all so stupid, that
can't be it. They must just get together and re-
hearse a lot.

So this poor guy's afraid to move, just petrified,
still as a deer caught in somebody's headlights. In
his mind he was already picking his teeth off the
floor. Then Asshole took a little swat at the back of
his head. That's when the guy on the next stool
stood up and said, real simple and real clear,
"Leave him alone."

This was just what Asshole came for. "You gonna make me, faggot?" he said.

But this was also where he made his big mistake. The guy he was talking to was a White Tower
regular everybody knew as Frank. And Frank was
not a faggot, but he *was* a full-blooded Lumbee Indian who had been fighting the white assholes
since he was knee-high to a duck.

"Yeah," Frank said and smashed that asshole's
nose like it was a ripe walnut ready for cracking.

Now I have been in bars, especially straight
ones, where one fight will break out and then half
a dozen more'll start up just like that, for no good
reason, just to be doing. But the White Tower that
night kept its cool. Joe and several more got up
like they might join in, but Frank didn't seem to

need any help. Asshole threw a couple of wild swings and took a few more punches in the face and chest. He was getting the shit beat out of him, is what it was. I hate to say I actually enjoyed it, but how could you not? Things were about to get dangerous, though. One more good punch, and Frank would've put him smack-dab through the plate-glass window.

So it was probably a good thing Hazel came charging out of the kitchen yelling, "Outside! You boys take that fight out of here right now!" And do you know they both snapped to and done it? Went right out that door, with Frank shoving and Asshole getting in a cheap shot to Frank's mouth in the doorway, but they went. Hazel's voice must've tapped into that part of both their brains that automatically kicked in and minded Mama, 'cause they were out in a jiffy. Which shifted the spotlight to Hazel. Everybody clapped and called her name. She blushed.

Outside, the fight was winding down. From where I sat you could see Frank had Asshole down on the hood of a blue Dodge Dart, just holding him there. While Joe was still up watching this, Lila scooted across the seat and got up. She'd had enough of it. "Boys will be boys. Excuse me, girls," she said, clutching her silver lamé purse, "I'm going to the powder room."

I looked at Rochelle then, expecting her to be really upset, but she wasn't. She had the calmest look on her face, downright peaceful, like what she'd seen was soothing as a damn Calgon bath. I can't explain it, but there it was.

"I believe I would like a piece of that pecan pie," she said to me.

Every time Frank started to let him up, Asshole'd swing at him again, and Frank would knock him back down. You know, boy shit. This went on for a while, till Frank finally turned him loose and he split back to his friends wherever they were or back to the rock he came out from under. I tell you one thing, he was beat up good. And I tell you another — he was gonna think twice before he fought any more faggots at the White Tower.

Meanwhile, Cora, who hardly ever said a word, stood in the doorway from the kitchen and made a whole little speech. "It's all right now, I called, and the police, they're on the way." She meant it to make everybody feel better, but her idea of the police and ours were nowhere near the same. And now Frank was outside by himself, looking around and touching his mouth to see if it was bleeding.

Joe leaned over our table. "I'll be back," he said. "I gotta get that guy outta here before the cops come. You know they'll haul him in for beating up a white boy." He lit out of there, calling over his shoulder, "I'll be back."

It was like watching mime, him going up to Frank, saying something, and pointing to his pickup. Frank looked back inside at the counter where he'd left half his burger, felt his lip, and decided not to finish it after all. The picked-on guy on the stool beside his pointed to Frank's plate, waved a bill, and said out loud, "I've got it." And as Joe's pickup pulled out, driving Frank to safety, the guy gave a little sigh and went, "My hero."

Maybe people were done eating, and maybe they weren't, but the place started to clear out pretty fast. Lila came back from the ladies' room just as Hazel was serving her French toast, but she didn't sit down.

"Where's Joe?"

"He's coming right back," Rochelle told her.

"Yeah," I said, "he took Frank somewhere so the cops wouldn't get him."

"Cops?" Lila gave a shudder. "This is all too much for me, honey. Me and cops just don't see eye to eye." She paused. "My daddy is a cop." And she scurried away, leaving her breakfast untouched, and got a ride with somebody in a white Pontiac Grand Prix.

"Well," said Rochelle, pulling off a bite of French toast, "what are we gonna tell Joe?"

That was the only sad thing about that night. Besides the fact that almost nobody got to eat their meal in peace. And besides the other fact that when we got back to her house, Rochelle drank straight whiskey till noon the next day because I guess she wasn't really as calm about all that violence as I thought she was.

But poor Joe. He was so disappointed. "Didn't you tell her I was coming back?" We said we did. He kept shaking his head and slapping his cap against his thigh. "Aw, shoot," he said, "damn. Try to help a fella out, and look what happens. I lose my drag queen." His eyes roamed the other booths, but it was just reflex — he knew she was gone. "Now don't that beat all?" he asked us.

Rochelle and me, we both agreed it did.

The View From Inside

by

Anne Seale

At this moment I am leaning against the cold concrete wall of a holding cell in the women's wing of
the city jail, soaking wet, holding on to my jeans
because they took my belt away. I have to stand
because the benches are full of my fellow lesbians,
also beltless and soaking wet, who are so pissed,
they won't shove over to let me sit down. Want to
know why?

It started in September, when against great odds
Marty Twigg and I became lovers. You see, she
isn't my type at all. I go for petite femmes usually, the lipstickier the better. Marty, however, is a
square, well-padded butch, a lot like me, only a
foot taller. And like me, she wouldn't be caught
dead in makeup. One of my greatest fears is that I
will die before my mother does, and when my
friends look into my coffin ready to cry or something, they'll fall on the floor and roll around hoot-
ing because Mom instructed the mortuary cos-
metician to give me the works. Marty feels that
way too.

We met when Marty started working where I
work, at Byron's Ambulance, and we found ourselves being partnered up a lot. Much of the am-

bulance business, especially on second shift, con-
sists of sitting around parked somewhere, waiting
for calls. So Marty and I had plenty of time to get
to know each other.

At the time I was living with Desiree Stenovic.
Desiree and I were having relationship troubles
due to the fact that she had developed a busy social life that didn't include me. Half the time she
wasn't home when I hauled in after work at midnight, and when she was, so were eight or nine
other people. When I finally moved out, it took
several days for her to miss me — and only then
because she went to my drawer to borrow my de-
odorant and it was gone. She's hardly spoken to
me since, but I don't know if it's because I left her
or because she had to go all day without underarm
protection.

It was Marty who saw me through the breakup;
in fact, it was Marty who urged me to break up
with Desiree in the first place. She said a gal as
sweet as me didn't need that kind of aggravation
and, by the way, she had a spare bedroom. I should
have suspected something right there.

As it turned out, I used the spare bedroom for
only a week, after which I was spending so much
time in hers that I moved in. Mine was made into
one of those fake bedrooms that are occupied only
when parents come to visit. "Why no, Mother, she
doesn't mind giving up her bed and bunking with
me at all!"

The View From Inside

Until then I thought if you didn't feel sexual sparks with a woman from the git-go, they would never develop. Wrong. In Marty's bed I changed my whole idea of what's titillating. In fact, to this day I can't think about Marty's big toe without a bunch of hormones going on a rampage throughout my system.

Our relationship was good in other ways too. Marty liked to do what I liked to do, eat what I liked to eat. We even watched the same TV shows: Oprah, Phil, and Rolonda but not Sally.

However, after seven months of cohabitational bliss, Marty and I broke up, and it was all because of the rabbit. Marty, big butch that she is, slept with a childhood toy, a two-foot-long stuffed rabbit that looked more like a dead opossum. Its matted fur had deteriorated to an uneven grayish brown, and the ears hung limply around a misshapen face that only a mother stuffed rabbit could love. Its name was Bunrab, and, frankly, Bunrab didn't smell too good.

This repulsive thing lay in bed with us every night. Marty tried to keep it on her other side, but often I would wake up to find it stuffed between us. I would then seize it by an ear and heave it under the bed, but the following night Bunrab would be back in the sack with us, peering at me through its one good eye, smirking.

I stood it with reasonably good humor because it was sleep with Marty and the rabbit or sleep alone in the fake bedroom. Then one day I came down with the flu and couldn't go to work. Marty fixed me Campbell's chicken noodle and tucked me into bed. She put Bunrab in next to me before taking off, telling the mangy thing to take care of me until she got back.

Of course, the first thing I did after hearing the garage door bang shut was grab an ear and toss Bunrab way under the bed. But maybe because I was already nauseous, the sourness floating up around the mattress seemed even less tolerable than usual. Then I got an idea.

I dragged Bunrab from the nether regions and padded on bare feet down to the laundry area. Dropping him in the washing machine, I added plenty of Tide and a dollop of Clorox before setting the water temperature on hot and turning it on.

After watching an old *Cagney & Lacey* rerun, the one where Cagney gets shot and Lacey blames herself and drives Harvey and everyone else nuts with her fretting, I returned to the laundry area and lifted the lid. At first I thought the creature must have escaped, because there was nothing in the machine. On looking closer, I saw bits of stuffing and pieces of light gray fur, one with a glass eye attached, plastered to the sides of the drum. I had to force myself to stick my hand in and scrape off what was left of Bunrab.

It was difficult packing with such a high fever, but I was motivated. I left a Baggie with Bunrab's remains in it on the kitchen table, put my jacket on over my pajamas, and left. I had already called and warned Mom that I was on my way.

So there I was, flat on my back in my old twin bed, searching for faces in the powder-blue paisley wallpaper like I used to do when I was a kid home sick from school. I even smelled just like I did then, since Mom insisted on rubbing my chest with Vicks VapoRub.

I missed Marty like crazy. On the second day I worked up enough courage to phone her. When Mom left for the drugstore to buy more Vicks, I went to the kitchen and dialed, but Marty wasn't home. She'd been there long enough, however, to take my name off her answering machine. I didn't try again.

On returning to work after being out for a week, I found that Marty had transferred to third shift. I never even saw her. By the time my new partner, Josh, and I got back to the garage at 11:30, she was already on the road.

After two months of being so down in the dumps that my mother threatened to make an appointment for me with her therapist, Dr. Gribbin, I decided I'd better get on with my life, maybe meet some new people. In other words, time to hit the Park 'n' Meter, our local women's bar.

So on my next weekend off, I called a few friends to see if anybody was interested in joining me for a drink. They were all deeply in love at the moment and couldn't make it, so I put on my best jeans and red wool sweater and set off by myself.

I was aware that it was Marty's weekend off and that she might be at the bar. I even knew there was a possibility that she might be there with a date. But that was a chance I had to take. *I can handle it,* I told myself.

The bar was still pretty empty when I arrived. I ordered a beer and was scoping for possibilities when Marty came in. She was with a date, all right, but it wasn't just any old date. It was *Desiree.* I couldn't believe it. My two most recent exes strutting in the door with their arms around each other, hips so tight, you couldn't slide a dental dam between them. They came up to the bar around the corner from me, moved two stools together, and proceeded to sit almost in each other's laps, flirting and laughing and glancing in my direction every once in a while like they were talking about me and wanted me to know it. They even had matching drinks, something pink with fruit.

Well, if I wasn't upset enough by the fact that they were in there together for all the world to see, I was driven to near panic when it occurred to me that they might be comparing notes about what it was like to live with me! My mind filled with gruesome images of things they might be saying.

"Does Chris still pour about a quart of milk on her Wheaties and wait till they turn to mush before she eats them?"

The View From Inside

"Yes, and don't you hate the way she sets the alarm for an hour before she has to get up and hits the snooze button about a hundred times?"

I couldn't even bear to think about what they might be sharing about my sexual performance. "Does Chris still…?" "Yes, and don't you hate the way she…?" I felt my ears turn red.

As if reading my mind, they started laughing and talking even louder, using cryptic hand motions now. I couldn't stand it. I had to go somewhere where I wouldn't have to watch. Grabbing my Bud, I slid off the stool and started edging by the two offenders, heading toward the pool room. When I was directly in back of them, Desiree turned.

"Why, Chris," she said. "Why didn't you tell me Marty's such a hot number?"

A hot number! Well, she is, but I sure didn't want to hear it from Desiree. I looked down at the bottle of beer clutched in my hand. I watched it rise into the air and pour its contents right on top of Desiree's thirty-dollar blow-dry.

Desiree shrieked and hurled her pink drink at me, spraying several women around me. They shrieked in turn and threw their drinks, creating more wet angry people, and so on. The bartender or somebody must have called the police, because about two dozen of us ended up being herded out and locked up together in this dismal cell.

So here I am, standing against the wall, an outcast. None of the other arrestees will talk to me or even look at me. On a bench to my right sit Marty and Desiree, side by side, wet and shivering. As I'm looking, Marty raises her eyes. There's such a sadness in them, and it's probably all my fault.

Suddenly I realize that the unthinkable is about to happen. Blobs of water are pushing up under my eyelids, and — oh, no! — they're oozing out. I turn to the wall so that no one can see, trying to wipe the tears away with the scratchy sleeve of my sweater. This is the last straw for me, the final humiliation. Tough little Chris is crying!

I feel an arm snake around me, and a damp Kleenex is stuffed into my hand.

"I'm sorry," Marty whispers in my ear. "I played a dirty trick, making you watch me cuddle with Desiree. I did it because I'm so angry with you."

"I'm sorry I murdered Bunrab, Marty," I sniff, not looking at her. "It was an accident."

"I know it was," she says. "Those loaded washing machines can be real dangerous. But that's not what I'm angry about."

Now I look at her. "It's not?"

"Oh, no. I'm angry because of the way you left me. You just walked out without a word. Without even waiting until I got home."

"I had to. I couldn't face you. I thought you'd hate me." As if it might make her feel better, I add, "I left Desiree like that too, you know. And Julie…and Michelle…and…" Who was before Michelle? Dixie? Jayne?

The View From Inside

"Then maybe you owe each one of us an apology…" Marty said.

"Each one of you?" Jeez, hope I haven't got anything else planned for the rest of this year.

"Starting with Desiree." She takes my hand and drags me over to where Desiree is sitting. Desiree sees us coming and makes a big show of being in a deep conversation with the woman next to her. We stand in front of her politely until she finishes and looks up. Marty nudges me.

"Desiree," I mumble, trying not to let anyone else hear. "I'm sorry for leaving you…like that."

"What?" Desiree says really loudly. "What did you say, Chris?" Everyone within ten feet of us looks our way.

I lean over a bit. "I'm sorry I left you like that… you know, without a word."

She gazes at me like I'm speaking Hindu or something, then says to Marty, "What's she talking about?"

"Chris is apologizing to you. She's trying to mend her ways. Tell her you forgive her."

Desiree looks around, happy with all the attention she's getting. "Sure," she shrugs, "why not?"

"And by the way, Desiree," Marty continues. "I'm breaking up with you, if that's okay, and going back to being lovers with Chris."

"You are?" Desiree and I say in unison.

I bury my face in Marty's neck. It smells like peppermint schnapps. Suddenly I don't care if I'm in jail or wherever, just so Marty's here with me. After a while I raise my head and say to her, "Can I come back?"

"To live with me? I don't know," she narrows her eyes and looks at me sideways. "Will you promise never to do that again? If we have problems, will you stay and talk, try to work them out?"

"I promise," I said, sealing it with a brief but potent kiss. As a playful afterthought I add, "And you know what, Marty? I'll even buy you a new bunny." I wait for her to laugh, but she doesn't.

"Okay," she says, "I think that's fair."

When they finally take us up for processing, I am still mentally kicking myself. No matter what the decision of the judge is, I have just sentenced myself to a life term of sleeping with an obnoxious two-foot stuffed rabbit. Sure hope I can find one.

She Called Me Jules
by
Julie Mitchell

We go out dancing every Friday night. Just the two of us. Two women. College best friends. Seniors, in the dance department. With boyfriends.

We are in sync. Make the same movements to the same music without plan. I turn around, open my eyes, see her torso, her hands, accenting the same beat as mine. Like our bodies are connected.

I start having uncontrollable dreams. About her. About us. Naked and touching. Erotic dreams that I don't understand. Don't want to stop.

We throw a party together. At her place. Lots of wine and candles, intense conversation, charged interactions.

I go to her room to change the CD. Enya. I lie down on the floor, buzzed and feeling sexy. She comes in. Lies beside me. Closes her eyes. Pulses. My heart pounds out rhythms in double, triple, quadruple time.

I have dreams about you, I whisper. About being with you. About touching you.

I've thought about you too.

Awkward silence. Shock. I can hardly think. We get up. Go back to the party. I fuck my boyfriend that night.

Julie Mitchell

From then on, though, there is this sweet, subtle tension. Pressing us in. Closer to each other.

She tells me about her new lingerie. Do you want to see it? She flirts. I'll model it for you. Ha, ha.

Another night. Up to L.A. for a concert. We're groupies of this all-boy band. I get drunk again. Driving home, windows down, music streaming by. I feel high. Powerful. Open. She drives.

I still dream about you.

What are we going to do about it?

I don't know.

At my place, we park. Our hug good-bye goes on and on. Longer than friends touch. Stretches beyond into some new, unspoken place. I want her to invite herself up. I want to ask her up.

We say good night.

I'm probably going to sleep with her. I tell him. The boyfriend. My lover. He knows, all along. That I think about women. That way. He knows.

Do you want to break up? Because I'm going to do this. With or without you.

I love you. I don't want to end. Just tell me, okay? Just tell me. If. When.

Okay.

I'm at her apartment. In her room. Talking. Dinner over, music weaving. She's sore. Too many rehearsals, dance classes.

Will you give me a massage?

On her bed. Lying facedown. I straddle her. Flowered, soft dress. Rayon. My hands meet her back. Push fingers into flesh, press deep into muscle. She moans. Moves. Reacts.

Soon we glide past massage into some wondrous other realm. She initiates. By responding. I follow. By initiating.

She pulls the dress off. Overhead. Only bra, slip left. No underwear on. Unhooks her bra. Back to me. I feel, caress, explore. She sighs, murmurs, lifts off her belly. I touch her breasts. Small. Soft. Hard.

Rolls over. Takes off my shirt. Suckles. Hands and mouth reading skin like Braille. Nipples run over nipples. (Never thought of that before!)

Our mouths connect. The first time. Shy smile. So soft, I say, never felt lips so soft. More smiles. Kisses.

Slip slides down. Naked. Before me. No hair. At all. She shaves. Down there. Her clit is big, close to her opening. Now I understand why she comes during penetration. Why I don't.

My hands know what to do. Over hips and ass, between knees and thighs. Fingers drawn to center. Her cunt slick and cushiony, sucking me in. First one, then two. Thumb on clit, a giant muscle craving contraction.

She starts calling out my name. Julie. Julie. Oh, Julie. I go crazy. Julie. Crazy, fast, and hard. Julie. Oh, yeah. Julie, Julie, Julie. Until she goes crazy. Once. Twice. Fast and hard. Jul...

Slow dance.

She unbuttons my pants. Touches me. A little. I don't come easily. I don't come now. She's getting tired.

I want to taste her. My dearest fantasy. Transform vision into experience of the flesh. I move back to her. On top. She stops me. It's late.

We hug, kiss. I'm not staying the night. Hug. She walks me to the door. Hug. Good-bye. Good. Bye. I smile all the way home. Can't wait to see her again. To touch her. Again. To go down on her. Again and again.

The next time we see each other, I am overflowing. One drop spills over.

I blurt it out. What now?

It was nice. The one time. I'm glad it happened, but I don't want more.

I say nothing. Because I want. More. Much. More. Like all the time.

We drift. Slowly. Apart. I'm frustrated and confused. She backs out of a piece I want to choreograph. A pas de deux. Woman to woman. Trying to put into dance what I can't put into words.

We graduate. My mom throws me a big party. She drives up. After, in the firelight, she's exquisite. I can't take my eyes from her. Her hips curve in a landscape of shadow, backlit. She's the sexiest thing I've ever seen. My boyfriend sits right there.

She stays over. In the same bed. I can't sleep for the distraction. Razor awareness. Shaking, I burn

She Called Me Jules

to touch her. Force myself not to. Regret it the next
morning. (Regret it the rest of my life.)
    I go to Europe. With him. Four months away.
Four postcards. To her.
    We see each other when I get back. Once. For
lunch. Then my phone calls, letters, met with silence. I despair. Feel utterly helpless. Wait. Finally she calls.
    What do I mean to you?
    I don't know.
    Think about it.
    She never responds.
    I start having bad dreams. Uncontrollable. She
haunts me. I dream of her more than anyone I've
ever known. For weeks. Months. Years. She appears.
At night. Seducing me, fading from my grasp, using
me, failing to recognize me, discarding me.
    Severe depression sets in. No job, breakup with
boyfriend, living with Mom. The transition blues.
I seek counseling. With a lesbian therapist. I come
out. And realize I loved her. Then spend months
getting over her. My ex–best friend. The dancer. A
straight woman.
    Two years later. I receive a letter. Apologizing.
She's in therapy, dealing with things, old things.
Me. She skirts the issue. In my opinion. Not one
mention of our lovemaking.
    I write back. Yes. I am a lesbian. Yes. I was in
love with you. Yes. You hurt me. I write for me. To
finish, finally.

Julie Mitchell

The dreams stop.

Three years after the letter. A holiday card. She still thinks of me. Wishes me the best. Hopes I'm doing well.

I never write back.

Shelling Peas
by
Merril Mushroom

The grandchildren and I huffed and puffed our way up the path from the garden to the house, hauling the weight of our harvest. We swung our buckets of peas through the kitchen door and plunked them down in the middle of the floor.

"Okay, Gramma Betts," piped Jossie, "here we are. Don't forget now, you promised."

"Right," I acknowledged. We picked up our shelling bowls and seated ourselves around the buckets, children on the floor and me on a chair. "Now," I said, "a story is what I promised, and a story you shall have." I scooped a double handful of pea pods into my bowl. "So what would you like to hear?"

"Um, um, um." Jossie, Cara, and Saroya made a big production about pretending to think. Then Saroya said slowly, as though they didn't predictably ask for the same story every time, "Um, tell us about you and Gramma Dee."

"Yeah, Gramma Betts," Cara elaborated, "tell us about the old days, you know, when you and Gramma Dee were little girls."

I settled back and started shelling my peas. "Long, long ago," I began, "in the old days, when

Gramma Dee and I both were little girls, Gramma Dee was what we called a tomboy." Jossie, Cara, and Saroya sat at my feet, squeezing fat green pods until they split, pushing peas into bowls, slight pinging sounds accenting the rhythm of my words.

"She hated wearing dresses," I said, "but she loved her dungarees."

"She loved her dungarees," Jossie repeated, giving a little sigh of pleasure. Jossie loved her dungarees too.

"She didn't like dolls. She didn't like to play house or school or nurse like the other girls. She preferred to be outside, climbing, running, playing ball, doing all the things that the boys liked to do. In those days it wasn't proper for girls to play like that. Girls were supposed to be quiet, sweet, gentle, and weak. Being a tomboy was acceptable as long as the girl grew out of it, but your Gramma Dee didn't show any signs at all of growing out of it — as a matter of fact, the older she got, the better she got at doing boy things.

"She had nothing in common with the other girls, and since her family wasn't rich, none of them had to be friends with her. They often giggled among themselves and made fun of her. One would think that being a tomboy, she'd have friends among the fellows, but a lot of the boys wouldn't play with her either, and her only real friend was her cousin Timmie."

Shelling Peas

"The boys were jealous of her," Saroya said sagely, "because she was better than they were at the things they liked to do."

"Yes," I smiled, "whatever she tried to do, she was good at it."

"And you, Gramma Betts. Tell about your limp now," Cara ordered, "about the accident."

I tossed spent pods into the bucket and took another lapful of peas to shell.

"I had an accident when I was very young. I got my foot crushed in a tobacco setter, and an infection set up in the bone so that my foot didn't grow right after that, and I walked with a limp. In those days having a limp caused a person to be pitied and stared at and left out. The other girls my age wouldn't play with me, especially because, besides the limp, my family wasn't rich and I was not a pretty little girl; and all of that was very important to girls my age back then."

The grandchildren interrupted at this point with loud chattering about how very beautiful I was and how stupid those girls were; and I knew I was the richest woman in the world!

"Okay, the story," Jossie demanded, getting us all back on track.

"I looked down on your Gramma Dee too," I continued, "because the other girls looked down on her, and I wanted to be like them. The other girls would mock her behind her back and bad-talk her among themselves; and my desire to be included among them was so great that I would join in, when I could, in making fun and saying the nastiest things of all. I never gave a thought to how Dee might feel from all this unkindness.

"Then one day after school, as I was heading across the play yard to go home, Percy Clarence and two of his tough friends cornered me by the fence in an area where the teacher couldn't see. Motioning to his friends that they should watch him, Percy came very close to me. 'Hey, Betts,' he sprayed spit on me when he spoke, 'did you see that walrus in the science film today? That's you! You walk just like that old walrus. Clump, clump, clump. C'mon, show us the walrus walk.' And he reached out and pushed me.

"'You leave me alone, Percy Clarence!' I started to cry.

"'Urk, urk, urk,' he grunted, and he pushed me again. I lost my balance and fell into the dirt. Percy Clarence and his friends roared with laughter, and he stepped up and started to kick me; but suddenly his laughter ended in a shriek. I clawed tears, sweat, and dust out of my eyes and looked to see what was happening."

"Gramma Dee!" the girls all cheered.

I laughed. "Yes indeed, Gramma Dee was clinging on to that bully's back and giving him quite a pounding. His friends tried to pull her off, but by then I had managed to get back up and found some stones and dirt clods to throw, distracting them.

Shelling Peas

Then the whole lot of them were in a heap on the ground with arms and legs flying, and before I knew it, Percy Clarence had broken loose and was running away crying, his two buddies behind him.

"Gramma Dee stood up. My, she was a mess! Her clothes were dirty and torn, and her face and hands were filthy and scratched and scraped. She looked down at herself. 'My mom's gonna kill me when she sees me,' she said. 'She warned me that if I got into another fight, she'd tan my britches good when I got home.'

"'You can come home with me,' I volunteered immediately, not really aware of what I was saying until the words were out of my mouth. 'It's just my mom and me that live there, and my mom is at work. You can clean up, and no one has to know about the fight.' Suddenly I felt very shy and warm and sort of furry inside. 'Hey, thanks,' I mumbled. 'You did that for me, and now you might be in trouble because of it.'

"Dee puffed up like a little rooster. She grinned broadly. 'Sure,' she said. Then, more seriously, she added, 'They deserved it. That was nasty and spiteful of them, picking on you that way. Besides,' she frowned, 'I owed that Percy Clarence one because I can't play football anymore. C'mon, let's go.'

"'What do you mean?' I asked as we left the schoolyard together. 'Why can't you play football anymore because of Percy Clarence?' I remembered seeing her play — it was one of the things the girls made the most fun of her about — and for some reason that memory made me feel like blushing.

"'Before Percy Clarence joined the team,' she said, and I could hear the rage contained in her voice, 'everything was just fine. I mean, none of the guys except Timmie liked me much, but at least they let me play, because they won more games when I did. But Percy Clarence thought it would be fun during practice to grab me on my parts whenever he could.' She touched her chest and then her straddle, and I noticed for the first time how tight her shirt stretched over her breasts. 'Just him alone I could have handled, but he told all the other guys they'd be cool to do it too. And they all went along with it, except for Timmie.' She shrugged. 'I got tired of fighting them, so I stopped playing football.'

"After that Gramma Dee and I became close friends. We were together all the time, either at her house or mine; and we even swapped seats in school so she could sit behind me." I stood up to stretch and empty pea pods into the compost.

The girls hadn't moved. "Okay, Gramma, now the sad part," called Cara. I sat down again.

"And then the happy ending," Saroya added quickly.

I cleared my throat. "One day my mom came home with the glorious news that she was going to marry the man she'd been dating and that we would move away and have a better life. She did not understand why I burst into tears, why I insisted I didn't want to leave. I tried to explain to her how much I loved Dee, how my heart would break to be away from her, but my mom told me that I'd make other friends, that Dee and I could write, and maybe we could visit one another. I just couldn't make her understand. We moved away, and my heart was broken.

"Dee and I exchanged a few letters, and then I didn't hear from her anymore, and my own letters were returned; and then Mom found out from one of her old friends that Dee took my leaving very hard, and finally her parents sent her to see a guidance counselor. He told them that Dee had an identity problem, that girls her age should have grown out of a tomboy stage by now, and that she was making too much of her separation from me. He recommended treatment for her. So her poor parents, believing in the voice of the 'expert,' had Dee locked away in a mental hospital for four years, where they gave her intensive psychotherapy and a lot of medication to try to cure her.

"When she got out, she came home and packed her things, and the very next day she left town and went to the big city and was not heard from again. But I didn't find out about that until much later."

I paused in a short reverie, until I was interrupted by Cara's reminder. "And you, Gram? Now tell us about you all this time when you didn't know about Gramma Dee."

"Poor Gramma was so sad," whispered Jossie.

"I thought that Dee had simply forgotten about me. Mama's new husband was a good man, and he took care of us. The years went by, and I graduated from high school and got a job.

"Then I met Eddie. I wanted to finally have a normal life, to have a husband and a house and children like all the other girls, so we married, and I had your mama." I looked at the girls and smiled, thinking how very worth it all, no matter what, this was. Then I continued, "But I started to have dreams about Dee almost every night, and she was often in my thoughts during the day. Finally I realized in my heart that it was her I loved and not Eddie. I knew I couldn't go on pretending, so I divorced Eddie, and your mama and I went back home to look for Dee. That was where we lost the trail. All anyone knew was that she had been in the mental hospital, came home, and immediately disappeared. No one, not even her family, had heard from her since then. They didn't even know if she was still alive.

"With the little money I had left, I got a small apartment in the city. I found a job, and I met a lot of other single mothers. Together we worked out a child-care exchange with each other. Through them I heard about a grant for single working mothers to take courses at one of the universities in order to be able to get a better job. The classes would be at night, and there was baby-sitting provided for our children. I applied and was accepted."

The peas were forgotten now as the story reached its high point. "Here comes the Judith part," Jossie announced.

"C'mon, Gram," Cara said impatiently. "Judith was a young woman in one of your classes…" she prompted.

"Yes," I said, picking up the thread of the tale again, "Judith was a young woman in one of my classes, and we became good friends. We got in the habit of eating supper together after class once a week. One evening she told me that she was a lesbian and that she lived with a girlfriend, not a boyfriend. She was tired of talking in code all the time to other people who she thought wouldn't be able to accept this — saying 'he' instead of 'she' and faking a name. She said she needed at least one person in her life with whom she could be honest, and she felt she could trust me.

"'So what's your girlfriend like?' I asked.

"Judith smiled at me warmly. She got this far-away look on her face. 'She's strong and brilliant and beautiful,' she said, 'and she sweeps me off my feet.'

"As I listened to Judith talk about her girlfriend, I found that my own thoughts had turned to Dee, and when Judith had finished talking, I looked away from her. 'I loved a girlfriend once,' I said, 'when I was young. Does that mean that I'm a lesbian too?'

"'How did you love her?' asked Judith.

"My words came unexpected, unplanned: 'I loved her from my heart, with all my heart; and she has remained forever in my heart.'

"'Come home with me,' Judith suggested, 'and meet my girlfriend. If you want, you can hang out with us and meet other lesbians. Then you can decide for yourself.'

"So I went to Judith's house for supper and met Katrina, and I felt very comfortable. 'There's a big lesbian picnic and softball game next weekend,' Katrina told me. 'Why don't you come with us?'

"'Don't you think it might be a little much for Betts to get that much 'exposure' right away?' Judith asked.

"'No, really,' I said, 'I'd like to go.' And so it was that the following weekend, I was in the car with Judith and Katrina on our way to City Park to join scores of other women who would be there for the big event."

We all had resumed shelling peas with vigor, and the excitement among my granddaughters was almost palpable as they anticipated the end of the story.

"I was feeling a little shy around so many women that I knew were lesbians, and I also was thirsty, so I went over to the soft-drink wagon to get a bottle of soda. A group of women stood nearby. They were talking together animatedly with great gusto and energy. Then one voice rose, and the others quieted, and suddenly my head started to spin until I thought that I would faint.

"My heart began to beat in rhythm with the patterns of the words and sentences that I was hearing. I listened intently, trying to figure out why I had been so ensnared by this conversation, which certainly was none of *my* business. There was something about the intonations, the sound of the words, the shapes of the syllables, that roused a feeling of déjà vu that caught me up to the exclusion of everything else. The voice got louder, raised in argument or announcement, and suddenly all pasts came flooding in on me, and my heart leaped. I looked about frantically for the speaker.

"There! She had her back to me and was waving her hands up and down in her argument. I recognized that gesture! Suddenly I knew! I raced over to where the women were standing..."

"The wings, Gran," interrupted Cara, "you left out the wings."

"Oh, yes — as though my feet had wings," I amended, "I raced over to where they were standing. I pushed through the women who were in front of the speaker, and at that moment she looked up and saw me."

The children were all leaning forward now. "Her face," Saroya blurted out, unable to contain herself.

"Her face changed. Oh, how it changed, an adventure to behold! Her words trailed off. Her eyes grew wide. Her face turned very white, then red. She squeezed her eyes shut and opened them again. She raised her hand to her brow. Then she jutted her head forward and looked squarely at me. 'Betts?'

"I could only nod my head, and then the growing lump in my throat exploded behind my eyes, and I burst into tears. And then we were in each other's arms."

"The end!" the girls chorused happily.

Just then the kitchen door opened, and none other than Dee herself came in, followed by Tara and Coddie. I looked at her affectionately — white hair, wrinkled face, crooked limbs. There was a smudge of dirt on her nose.

"Gramma Dee hit a homer," Coddie announced.

"Well, maybe I can't run the bases like I used to," Dee grinned, "but I can still give that ball a good clobber."

"Some things never change," I chuckled, and we all burst out laughing.

Muffie's Midnite Lounge, 1958

by
Cathy Cockrell

"What about them Yankees?!" Three games into the World Series, the little mob man with the caterpillar eyebrows was itching to talk baseball. And here sat Dana in her Brooklyn Dodgers shirt, in no mood to chitchat with a fool. The Dodgers had just finished their first season in L.A. And now Petite had left her too.

"She don't want to talk," Bo told the man. Dana was a wreck. Any saphead could see that.

The mafia man took a drag off his king-size cigarette and exhaled his wounded pride in the direction of the dance floor, where couples circled to another moody slow song.

And with the most fervent desire of my soul, Bo remembered from her catechism, *I pray and beseech you...don't let Dana start to cry.*

"Come on, Dana," Bo implored. "You got to snap out of it."

"Why do I got to?"

"I just wish you would, that's all. Look at all these women!"

"Give me a break. A person has food poisoning, and you tell her to eat."

Cathy Cockrell

Dana was right. It *was* a stupid thing to say. Bo had never liked the way Dana played the femmes on the sly. At least now she was remorseful. But Dana in splinters was disturbing.

"You know what I want?" Dana bent her index finger at a right angle so that it pointed through the table to the basement. Down in the basement was a crowd that bought and sold reefer, black beauties, even heroin. The first time Bo had ever shot horse was downstairs, locked in one of the johns.

"Gotta take a pee. Don't let anyone take our table," said Dana for the benefit of the mob man. He sat on a stool in the back of the bar, the heels of his shiny black shoes hooked on a horizontal rung. He kept an eye on the restless natives.

Bo watched Dana disappear through the doorway that led down the steep stairs. Dana and Petite had been like parents to her. When she was thirteen they had introduced her to the life. She was nineteen now. She had taken for granted that Petite and Dana would be together forever.

Bo fiddled with the matchbook in the ashtray, opening and shutting the cover. It read MUFFIE'S MIDNITE LOUNGE on the front side, THE GAYEST SPOT IN NYC on the back.

"A quarter-carat diamond! That's easily $300!" said the woman at the next table.

"No way. Maybe a really excellent gem. A quarter carat you can get for as little…"

Muffie's Midnite Lounge

Bo missed the minimum price for such a stone as the opening bars of "All Shook Up" rose from the speakers and the dance floor filled up again. She heard someone say her name. Bo turned, felt her heart catch. Tall Nicky from Delancey Street stood beside her, grinning a too-tight smile, a Rheingold in each hand. Nicky had been a chum of Bo's big sister; she'd been wild like Mo, but she'd survived. She wasn't with Maureen the day she disappeared. Seeing Nicky was always bittersweet.

"You bum! Pull up a seat."

Tall Nicky fumbled with the chair. She was a bit gilded already. She was called Tall Nicky 'cause there were others with the same name, like Pony Tail Nicky from Hell's Kitchen.

"Where's your soft spot?" asked Bo.

Nicky looked away and took a pull of beer.

"Oh, no, not you too! You and Bernice split up again?"

Nicky nodded, raised her fingers — four of them — and said, "Third time." Bo folded down the fourth finger. Nicky looked only a little sheepish as she said, "Three's the charm. Looks like this time it's for good."

Bo didn't want to hear the story — not tonight. Luckily, Nicky didn't seem to want to tell it. "You look like Little Miss Lonely yourself, back here in the corner."

"I'm waiting for a friend," Bo lied. "What else you up to, Nicky?"

"Still driving."

Bo remembered: Nicky worked out of the same garage as Dana, or used to; Dana had switched outfits. The one where Nicky still worked was full of alkies.

"I'm sick of working for assholes. I want my own medallion."

"Taxi medallions cost a bundle. You know that. How many women you know got medallions?"

Nicky ignored her question. "Saving my dimes is never gonna make it!" She struck the table with her fist.

"You need a scheme or a scam," Bo laughed. She needed one herself.

"I'm serious, Bo. I'll consider anything. Dealing, the sex trade, anything."

Bo looked at Nicky. She was not bad-looking, if she cleaned up her act a little.

Bo said, "I got some ideas there."

"You do?"

"No, I'm only kidding."

"You got some information, I can tell." Nicky aimed her finger at Bo.

"Well, I do know of one possibility."

"Turning tricks?"

"No, it's more in the line of theater. You really interested? I thought you said you were tired of assholes."

"If I've got to deal with assholes, I'd rather it paid decent."

Bo arranged three empties into a little family at the center of the table. "There's this guy on Canal. He's looking for people."

"People?"

"Women."

"What's the pay?"

"Hundred dollars a shot," Bo told her.

"Jesus! Where do I sign up? Is it porn movies?"

"Not exactly." Bo paused. "You fake a scene with a married man."

Nicky seemed unfazed, then said, "So he can get a divorce."

"Right."

"You doing that, Bo? You are, aren't you?"

"I did a few times," Bo said, lying. She wanted it to be only a few times, but it was more. She could say the photographer was a slime bag, but it was obvious Nicky was going to pursue this thing, regardless.

Nicky took a pack of Lucky Strikes from her shirt pocket and teased out a cigarette. She didn't bother to offer one to Bo. That seemed unlike her.

"Details!" Nicky demanded as the end of her cigarette caught the flame from her match.

Bo had the phone number in her red squeeze coin purse. But neither of them had anything to write with. She had to ask the stool pigeon to borrow his pen. As she reached out to take it, he held on, so she had to pull. Little bastard. She hoped he would end up in the East River with cement boots.

She copied the number and name onto a paper napkin.

"Maybe I'll send a print to Bernice," Nicky laughed bitterly as she folded the napkin and slipped it in her pocket.

"That, my dear, is a sick form of revenge."

Nicky took a pull of beer. "You know when me and Bernice first met?"

Bo wondered what it was about herself: In reform school, the bars, everywhere she went, people wanted to tell her their very private troubles. Usually she didn't mind.

"Nineteen fifteen!"

"I think you mean 1950," Bo offered.

"Right. We were just kids. I had a boyfriend back then."

"Honey! That *was* a long time ago."

Nicky started to remind Bo about that summer, but she didn't need to. Nineteen fifty was the year Maureen disappeared, the year she was sixteen and Bo eleven. Once, early that year, they ran into Nicky as they were coming out of the Elysian Fields Funeral Parlor. Maureen was embarrassed. She said something to make it seem that this was her little sister's dumb idea. What was so embarrassing, anyway? They had snuck in through an open window and combed the hair on a corpse that was laid out for a wake. So big deal.

"That was the year Bernice and I..." Nicky was saying.

Dana had not come up yet from the basement. She was having herself a grand old time. Bo wanted to go find her, but she had made a resolution: No more drugs; find a nice, steady woman who was not into all that. Look what drugs had made of her sister and of that drag queen who OD'd last weekend in the alley back of the Rendezvous. She was not going downstairs again. But she couldn't stay to be reminded of her sister either.

"Nicky, you got to excuse me awhile."

"No problem." Bo saw Nicky's fist tighten around her beer bottle. "I'll watch your jacket," Nicky volunteered.

Bo thanked her. She stood and pushed her chair against the table.

"The one with the limo? She's here?" one of the gem experts at the adjoining table was saying.

Bo picked a path through the crowd as Pat Boone crooned "Love Letters in the Sand." How Maureen had hated Pat Boone! A group of women at the edge of the dance floor were singing the words theatrically, with harmonies and everything. Nice that they were having fun, but there were better songs.

With her back to the crush of women — the mournful, jealous, horny, giddy, and tipsy — Bo stared down into the jukebox at the song names: "Honeycomb," "Bye Bye, Love," "Get a Job," "Yackety Yack." Yackety yack was right! Pieces of conversation floated on the air like motes of dust:

"I'm on a girl spree..."; "Kahlua, vodka, and cream..."

Bo dropped her coin in the slot and plugged the numbers for "The Pretenders" and "Thing of the Past."

"No, I swear it's her. Over there!" she heard someone saying.

Bo looked where the woman pointed — at a woman in a white coat, near the bend in the bar. Strange thing was, she was looking back. There were rumors about that woman. People said she was a madam. They said she came to Muffie's to recruit girls for her stable. It was news whenever she arrived. As soon as her chauffeur double-parked outside, the bouncer in the entryway would whisper something to, say, a woman in a soft sweater and Peter Pan collar standing just inside the inner door. The news would be on its way down the bar by the time the red lightbulb flashed on above the entrance, bathing the stranger in a ruby-colored glow. Sometime after midnight she might leave, with a girl or two, in her flashy limo. Then you wouldn't see her face again for a while.

Bo probed a sore spot next to one of her back molars with the tip of her tongue as she purposely avoided the woman's gaze. She leaned back casually against the wall to watch the show. A woman was giving her partner a tonsillectomy in the corner. An extremely nervous colored girl with a bright orange headband and shoulder-length straightened hair sat alone at one of the round tables to the right. Now the passionate kissers had stopped kissing, and one of them was mixing her drink with her finger.

The red light blinked on, then off, at the entrance. Dumb light. It wouldn't save anybody's skin. Its real purpose was to make everyone more uneasy so they'd buy more drinks. That was Bo's theory. If the politicians, papers, or cops really wanted some arrests, there would be a stampede to the fire exit. Outside, a fortunate few might get away. The cops would make the rest line up. Then pop, pop, pop, flashbulbs and racy captions. Women dressed like men sold lots of papers.

Someone like the bartender, who had a bleached blond DA and a dazzling tattoo of a mermaid on one shoulder, was the newspapers' perfect weirdo. Her name was Mona, but everyone called her the Mona Lisa. Never mind that Mona regularly took communion and made wooden lamps as a hobby. Or better still that she did.

Sometimes straights came in to see the freak show. They nursed their drinks and watched. "Is my head on crooked?" Bo had taken to asking. Not that those in the life wore the white hats. Caged rats got vicious.

Bo reached to the rim of her socks for her cigs, but she had left her pack at home. She went over to the bar, where Mona Lisa was scooping ice into drink glasses.

"Can I mooch a cigarette?"

Before Mona could answer, the woman on the last bar stool placed her fingers on Bo's wrist and handed her a cigarette. "Are you new in the Village?" It was the woman in the white coat. Some chivalrous butch must have sacrificed her seat.

Bo looked at the cigarette, momentarily confused as to how to get it lit.

"I just got back from upstate," she heard herself say in response.

"What took you upstate?" The woman twisted a strand of black hair around her index finger. Her hair was long and fell over her shawl collar. The collar, Bo saw, was part of the coat. She had a slender nose and a birthmark by her mouth like Marilyn Monroe. High-class.

"Reform school," Bo answered. She could have lied. Or she could have told another version of the truth: that she had gone to reform school a few years ago and a lot had happened since. The woman gave Bo a slow, steady look with her eyes. Dana used to look at Petite that way sometimes. Bo still wanted to believe in such looks.

"I find that interesting," the woman told her.

Bo smiled. That could be taken as a come-on. Not that it mattered. Women were constantly coming on to each other, falling in love, breaking up, and starting over again with someone new.

"I heard about you," Bo told her.

Muffie's Midnite Lounge

"Really? What did you hear?" The woman scratched her wrist with long painted fingernails.

"A few things. Among them that you were interested in me."

"Do you believe that?"

"I notice you're talking to me." Bo rocked gently back and forth on her hips.

"I talk to a lot of people."

This woman was the kind who wouldn't give an inch. The sudden image in Bo's mind was of that perfect white coat rubbing against the wall of the alley back of Muffie's as Bo reached under the woman's blouse. For the split second that the fantasy lasted, the woman wasn't smooth or haughty; it was Bo in control. Then it melted. She worried at that sore spot with her tongue.

Mona placed a drink in front of the woman — a clear drink with a squeeze of lime on the rim. The plastic swizzle stick had a poodle dog on the handle. The woman began stirring it slowly through the ice.

"Pauline," she said, as if her name were the answer to a riddle. "And you're...?"

"Bo."

Pauline offered her hand. They shook hands.

"The truth is, Bo, you remind me of someone."

"I do?"

"Someone I knew a very long time ago. You're her spitting image. I've been watching you. You think a lot, I see."

"You mean when I was over by the jukebox?" Bo felt herself less hard.

"I watched you watching people on the dance floor. You had your arms crossed in front of your chest, like this. I saw your little wheels going. Which intrigues me. I always want to know what people are thinking."

"I was watching two women kiss. I was wondering what it feels like to have a woman's tongue down your throat one minute and then she's talking about White Russians the next."

Pauline laughed. "I think you know. You're not innocent. If you were innocent, you wouldn't have looked so sad — like you were missing someone."

Bo didn't like having her feelings exposed like laundry on a line. "Is the woman I remind you of sad?" she asked.

"Was sad. At the end she was."

Had she gotten Pauline wrong? Maybe she too would love a good cry on Bo's shoulder?

"It is sad," Bo agreed.

"What's 'it'? This little dive you gals come to? Or do you mean life?"

Bo noticed the woman next to Pauline eavesdropping. "This is getting a little deep," she said.

"You've aroused my curiosity," Pauline told her. "But we have time. May I buy you a drink?"

Bo ordered a beer. There was that confidence of Pauline's again: *We have time.* And something else she'd said that was troubling: *This little dive you gals come to.* Bo wanted to go back in her mind to the alley, to finish what she'd started, but she couldn't hold on to the fantasy. Something was shifting inside her.

Pauline's coat was open in front. She wore a sheer black blouse with a black bra underneath. The rock on her right hand was black in a silver setting. There was something cold and fascinating about her. She stirred her drink and studied Bo.

"Would you care to dance?" Pauline offered.

What people said was true, then, Bo decided: Pauline *was* interested.

"If you like." Bo was supposed to do the asking. Pauline broke all the rules.

"Cool as a cucumber!" Pauline clucked. She asked a butch with red hair, who was standing behind her, if she would mind holding the coat and clutch bag. She entrusted her valuables to a stranger. Pauline wore black silk slacks and black seam stockings you could see at the ankles.

Bo followed the ankles out to the dance floor. Once upon a time Petite had taught Bo how to lead, to a ballroom dancing record, and Dana had coached from the couch. Bo did her best now as they box-stepped through a medium-tempo number.

Pauline was so fine. Did she go for women, or was this only part of her job like people said?

The song ended. They went back to the bar. The butch hopped off Pauline's stool and handed back the coat and clutch bag. Pauline pecked her a thanks on the cheek.

"What are you drinking?" Pauline asked. The woman said Johnnie Walker. Pauline beckoned Mona over with a lift of her chin. "Make her another Johnnie Walker, would you?" The butch looked disappointed, despite the free drink, as if she hadn't meant to serve as a hired aide but instead had been a contender for Pauline's interest. Pauline eased her bottom up onto the stool again and draped the coat over her lap.

"Anything you want, Bo?"

Was there a second meaning to that question, or did it only seem that way? Bo took a look in the direction of the disappointed butch to decide if there might be trouble. But she had already disappeared into the crowd.

Pauline had a second vodka gimlet. Bo finished her beer. What could she say to Pauline? She angled her body toward Pauline to express her interest but looked away, toward the crowd. Across the dance floor she caught a glimpse of the mobster's balding head. Had Dana returned yet from the basement? Were Dana and Nicky sharing their sorrows with each other? She hadn't expected to miss her friends.

Pauline handed Mona a crisp, freshly minted bill. The number in the corner by Pauline's thumb was 100. The photographer in the Canal Street loft had paid Bo each time with five twenties.

Once Dana had had a fifty, and she let Bo inspect both sides. Bo wondered how many more hundreds Pauline had.

"Have anything smaller?" asked Mona. The woman on the stool to Pauline's right was staring. Bo felt important and inadequate all at once.

"See what you can do. Four twenties would be fine," Pauline told her.

Bo quickly counted four drinks — her own, Pauline's two, and the one for the woman who'd held Pauline's coat — that Pauline was paying twenty dollars for, after change. Mona must welcome Pauline's visits. Bo caught Pauline eyeing her, as if all these calculations were showing.

Pauline opened her clutch purse and poked around till she produced a small mirror. She inspected her face, adding fresh red lipstick. She pressed her lips together to spread the lipstick evenly. She dropped the mirror back inside and clicked shut the bag.

Bo was not surprised when Pauline said suddenly and bluntly, "Would you like to go home with me?"

Bo's voice was quiet and very controlled: "I promised myself that if I ever turned a trick, I'd keep my own money."

"I was thinking," said Pauline, "more in terms of your going home with *me*."

"As you like," Bo agreed. The words came out evenly, lightly, but her heart was pounding. Would

Pauline be considered a nice, steady woman? She was very pretty.

"My, so cool!" The smile that spread across Pauline's face was that of a woman patting the head of a dog.

The woman next to Pauline turned to her neighbor. The second woman's face bobbed forward at the bar to get a look at Bo and Pauline.

Bo briefly remembered her jacket and the two friends she'd left in the back of the bar as she stepped outside of Muffie's into the cold night air.

Pauline opened the door of the waiting limousine — dramatically, Bo thought. But Pauline would seem dramatic no matter what. Everything about her was black elegance: her hair and clothes, the chauffeur's uniform, the limousine's black leather seats. The chauffeur didn't turn around to see the good-looking women he was transporting.

Ever since she was a kid, Bo had been called a looker. Looks could take you places, like Lana Turner being discovered at a lunch counter. She wished Petite could see her now. But not Dana, who for all her two-timing was a prude. She wished she'd see her sister on the curb, with her mouth dropping open and her boyfriend, Wilson, on her arm. She wished Sister Mary Martha, the meanest sister in grade school, vowed to chastity and poverty, would be at a crosswalk when they stopped at a light; Bo would roll down the window and throw her a casual hello, Pauline-style.

Muffie's Midnite Lounge

But by the time they hit the northbound lane of East River Drive, her images of the awed and envious were overwhelmed by the smell of leather and perfume and the sound of the tires. She needed to think fast and hard. They whooshed onto the 59th Street Bridge and into Queens. As the limo hit a rise in the boulevard, she caught sight, through the rearview mirror, of the glistening lights behind.

Members of the Wedding

by
Judith Stein

When she first entered the cinder-block gals'
room, Mollie saw only the crush of high-heeled
women in competing colognes, each intent on her
task with combs or cosmetics. Then the haze of
hair spray and cigarette smoke lifted, and Mollie
spotted her lover. Naomi was sobbing, hunched
over on the gold Naugahyde couch, oblivious to
the tapping high heels of the other wedding guests.
Pushing gently through the crowd, Mollie wondered, *Was the whole trip leading up to this?*

From the moment they had landed in Nashville,
Mollie wondered if they were in some kind of al-
ternate-reality amusement park. It started with that
accent, blurred to a murky drawl by the airport
loudspeakers and Mollie's blocked ears. At the
rental car counter, she and Naomi faced a familiar-
looking row of highly polished, smiling women,
each with hair bigger than the next and teeth the
size of small refrigerators. Smiling mercilessly,
the clerk told them that the agency was out of
compact cars and offered them what sounded like
a "fool-sized four-door." Then, just to confirm that
they had left behind their known universe, there
was no schlepping onto a minibus to the car rental

parking lot — Mollie and Naomi just walked out the door next to the rental counter to find their "fool-sized" car.

Instead of their usual tiny-mobile, Naomi and Mollie were given keys to a maroon vinyl-topped sedan as large as a pontoon.

"Now this is a car for women our size!" Naomi crowed. She and Mollie slid happily onto the burgundy crushed velvet seats and sat giggling for a full five minutes before they drove off. Every button, lever, knob, and handle had to be pushed, turned, cranked, and tested. Mollie finally managed to croak, "I'm starving, let's get dinner," between giggles, so Naomi started the car, gunned the engine, and pulled out of the parking lot onto the streets of Nashville.

Mollie and Naomi had four days before Naomi's brother's wedding. In full vacation mode they tootled happily around Nashville. Anticipating their return to Boston, they bought fabulous souvenirs for each of their friends. Music Row was perfect: a strip-mall shrine to schlock with identical ashtrays, toothpick holders, and laminated guitar-shaped burl-wood wall clocks differentiated only by the face of the particular country music star mounted on them.

Mollie was crazy about the Barbara Mandrell Music World's "You Too Can Be a Star" recording studio (only $49.95 for a six-minute recording). But Naomi's favorite spot was the Parthenon.

Judith Stein

Constructed for the 1896 World Exposition, Nashville's Parthenon was built exactly two thirds the size of the original.

Better even than the Parthenon was the 21-foot statue of Athena.

"Look, dear," Naomi crowed, "lesbian culture!"

Although she quibbled with Naomi over whether the Parthenon was superior to Music Row, Mollie secretly felt that Nashville's finest sight, the very pinnacle of civic pride, was the string-tie–wearing white man who picketed the statue of Athena with a sign that read, DESTROY HEATHEN IDOLS. PRAY TO JESUS CHRIST TODAY!

"That's devotion to a cause," Mollie commented when she learned from the hot dog man that the protester was there every day of the year and had been for at least six years.

"Except Christmas," the hot dog man added earnestly.

Mollie gave an "of course" kind of nod as she struggled to keep a straight face. Repeating that conversation to Naomi, she had expected shared amusement. Instead, Naomi scowled, fiddled with the Jewish star she always wore, and mumbled something about their plane having really landed on Mars.

By their second day in Nashville, Mollie had learned to ask for tea when she wanted iced tea and had learned to ask first if it had been sweetened. A lot of people seemed unable to understand

Members of the Wedding

Naomi's rapid-fire New Jersey accent. Sometimes Naomi repeated herself, trying to speak more slowly. Other times she just turned in frustration to Mollie, whose flat Midwestern accent allowed her to interpret Naomi's speech.

Mollie loved the food in Nashville, thanking her Indiana upbringing for her decidedly un-Jewish love of pork. She was delighted to eat barbecue at every meal and looked forward to eating vegetables cooked with ham. Naomi, touchy stomach already reflecting the tension she felt on this trip, was craving salad. By the third day both of them really wanted a bagel. They tried to find a Jewish deli but gave up after asking three different people, including a cabbie.

The day before they left Nashville to go to Michael's wedding, Mollie and Naomi went to the Loveless Motel and Café to eat fried chicken for breakfast. The idea of chicken at 8 A.M. was strange, but the reality was delicious. Eight pieces and twelve biscuits later, they packed their leftovers in a sack (no one there understood Mollie when she asked for a bag) and headed for Apex, the tiny hometown of the bride.

That first day in Apex, Michael and Laurie Ann, the bridal couple, took Michael's family to lunch. Michael's family was small — just Naomi and Mollie and an older sister, Sarah. Sarah, her husband, Robbie, and their daughter, Ruthie, had just arrived from Berkeley that morning. Laurie Ann's mother, Nancy, also joined them for lunch. Nancy, a smiling, down-to-earth woman, seemed utterly unfazed at having lesbian in-laws. She spent most of the lunch trying to see if she had any musical tastes in common with Mollie and Naomi; her most recent concert venture had been to see Eric Clapton two nights earlier. While they didn't find any musical overlap, Nancy's genuine interest in their lives was a pleasure.

At lunch both Nancy and Laurie Ann chatted about life in small-town Tennessee and how different it must seem from Boston or Berkeley.

"Everyone's being very nice," Sarah said nervously, repeating herself a few times as if that mantra could protect her hippie-looking family from the cold stares their group was starting to get. Since people sometimes gawked at them at home in Boston, Mollie was trying not to get too concerned.

Sarah's husband, Robbie, a veteran of Freedom Summer, was more blunt: "I said I'd never come back to the South. I can't believe I'm here. I hate it here. Let's just get this wedding over with so we can go home."

Robbie's comment stopped all conversation at the table. Flustered, Sarah said, "Oh, Robbie!" just as Nancy turned to Laurie Ann and asked brightly, "Are those orchids all set for Saturday?" Politeness was restored, and the meal concluded on a cheery note.

Members of the Wedding

By the morning of their second day in Apex, the stares were impossible to ignore.

"Not too many fat spiky-haired dykes in Apex," Naomi muttered after the seventeenth long hard look before 10 in the morning.

"Maybe they can tell that we're lesbians," Mollie observed.

"Or Jews," Naomi growled from between clenched teeth.

Already anxious at being in such a small town, Mollie toyed with one of her graying curls. At least Naomi had a clear purpose as the sister of the groom. Mollie simply tried to smile at the inevitable eyebrows raised when they answered the constant query "Where you gals from?" with "Boston." She always added that they were in Apex for a wedding, Laurie Ann Ridder — she'd grown up there. Did the hard-staring store clerk, waitress, desk clerk know her? No? Oh, well, her mom had moved up to Springville a few years before, and Laurie Ann? Well, Laurie Ann had been in Dallas for eight years now. That's where she met the groom. No, he wasn't from Texas; he was from New Jersey. More than one person responded with something like "Oh, a Yankee," as if that explained everything.

"So now I'm a Yenkee," Mollie had mused in a fake Yiddish accent, painfully aware of how un-Yankee she was in Boston. She had thought that chatting about the wedding with the townsfolk would provide an acceptable explanation for why they were in Apex.

Naomi didn't think that her brother's wedding bought them any credence at all. "We're such foreigners here" she said. "I don't feel safe. I keep waiting for the Klan to come riding through town. Even Sarah and Robbie are getting strange looks, and they're your basic married couple with two-point-five kids."

That night, as they lay in bed in Apex's only motel, Mollie tried to get Naomi to relax.

"Thank God your family is progressive," she started. "At least I know they won't harass us. And your sister understands why weddings are hard for us." At Naomi's murmured agreement, Mollie continued. "Look, Laurie Ann doesn't seem homophobic. And Nancy's really okay too."

She and Naomi had been ready to fight to be included as a couple in the wedding festivities. Their circle of friends was full of horror stories about someone's lover not being invited or getting seated separately from the family, and the stories even included one in which the family arranged a male date for the bride's lesbian sister and just happened to forget to tell her.

But so far Laurie Ann and Michael had done everything right. Mollie would be escorted to the groom's family pew and seated next to Naomi. She had even been invited to the ladies-only luncheon for the bride's large extended family. Secretly Mollie was almost disappointed that she was being treated so well. A good political fight would have relieved some of her anxiety.

"I wonder if Laurie Ann has told her family that we're lesbians," she mused quietly.

"I hope she has!" Naomi snapped. "Let her deal with some homophobia for a change." Naomi moved closer to Mollie, mashing their large soft bodies together. Stroking Mollie's arm, Naomi calmed down. "I know I should appreciate being included so completely, but I hate weddings. I don't care how much people smile here, I don't trust them one bit. They would never come to our wedding, if we could even have such a stupid thing. And we've been together seven years — no one except Nancy has asked one single word about our lives. We'd never get this kind of recognition, even if we were together seventy years. Hetero-sexual privilege, that's all it is!"

Mollie nodded agreement as she rubbed Naomi's shoulders. "Look, sweetie," she began softly, "we went through all this when you were deciding whether or not to come to the wedding. It seemed important to improve the connection with your family. I know it's not fair that we could never have this, but I'm trying hard to hold on to some shred of positive attitude to get me through. Can you try to remember why we came?"

"I'll try," Naomi answered grudgingly, "but it's harder than I expected. Well, I'm a big tough dyke;

I can get through this…" Naomi's voice trailed off into soft snores.

Still tense, Mollie lay awake thinking about the life she and Naomi lived. She couldn't wait to get home. *How do gay people live in places like this?* she wondered as she remembered her decision to leave Indiana. Finally she drifted off to sleep.

The next day was the ladies' luncheon. Since Laurie Ann lived in Dallas but wanted to get married in her hometown, her cousin Marcelle had planned the wedding. Laurie Ann had blathered on about how much Marcelle had done; this ladies' luncheon was Marcelle's special gift to the bride.

Although Mollie and Naomi arrived right on time with Sarah and her twelve-year-old daughter, Ruthie, most of the bride's family were already there. Marcelle's house was an enormous split-level — half of her den easily held the ten peach-and beige-covered card tables. Naomi and Mollie entered the den behind Sarah and Ruthie. Both of Laurie Ann's grandmothers were seated with Laurie Ann and her mother at the luncheon's equivalent of a head table. As Laurie Ann introduced her guests to her grandmothers, the grandmas smiled at Sarah and Ruthie. Mollie and Naomi got hard stares. One grandma muttered, "Fat Yankees," not quite under her breath. Behind Mollie, Naomi stiffened. Then she gave the grandmas what Mollie called a Miss Manners smile.

Members of the Wedding

"That's right, grandma," Naomi replied a little too loudly, "we're big fat women from the North."

As Naomi and Mollie made their way to their table near the kitchen door, Mollie breathed a sigh of relief that the explosion had been minor. She and Naomi were seated with Marcelle and Cousin Nancy, called that by everyone to distinguish her from Laurie Ann's sister, Nancy, and from her mother, Nancy.

"They couldn't think of another girl's name?" Mollie whispered to Naomi to try to lighten the mood. Tight-jawed, Naomi simply shrugged as the muttering grandma said grace. Naomi and Mollie choked on amen-ing a grace that thanked "our one and only Lord, Jesus Christ."

Ruthie stage-whispered, "Ooh, Mom, don't they know we're Jewish?" to Sarah, who shushed her quickly.

Mollie ate carefully, working to remember her company manners. She could tell Naomi was concentrating on the same task. Idly Mollie wondered who invented the silly foods served at meals for ladies. Keeping with the beige-and-peach color scheme of the wedding, they were served a beige cream of mushroom soup and tiny sandwiches of apricot jam on whole wheat bread.

Cousin Nancy was actually rather entertaining, telling them stories of all the places she'd lived as a Navy wife and about how Navy wives hated their husbands' constant presence in retirement. Both

Mollie and Naomi nodded politely at all the right places; Marcelle, who'd grown up with both Cousin Nancy and Mother Nancy, made smiling nasty digs at Cousin Nancy at every opportunity.

Suddenly Cousin Nancy turned directly to Naomi and asked, "What's the difference between parsley and pussy?"

Naomi made a small choking sound as Mollie blushed violet-red. Marcelle, enjoying this new diversion, laughed, "Oh, Nancy, you nasty thing," while Cousin Nancy looked at Naomi for an answer to her riddle. When it became clear that there was no way she could avoid this minefield by smiling stupidly, for no matter how long, Naomi finally got her wits together to croak out a "What?"

"No one eats parsley," Cousin Nancy crowed in triumph, clearly enjoying her ability to shock them. As Marcelle hurriedly excused herself to check on dessert, Mollie looked around to see if anyone else in the room had heard Cousin Nancy's rather loud query. Everyone seemed to be calmly finishing up their mandarin-orange-and-cashew salads ("As close to peach and beige as I could get," Marcelle had explained); Laurie Ann was playing proper guest of honor and circulating among the various tables.

The rest of the luncheon passed in a blur. Naomi was scowling; Mollie kept trying not to giggle. Finally they could leave. Driving back to the motel,

Members of the Wedding

Mollie and Sarah tried to figure out if Cousin Nancy was being crude because she knew she was seated with lesbians or because she was drunk on the champagne punch or just for the hell of it. Pontificating in her usual big-sister way, Sarah thought that Cousin Nancy was probably just participating in the long-standing tradition of Southern women's bawdy humor. Ruthie had no interest in adult explanations; she thought the joke was the funniest thing she'd ever heard and kept repeating it to herself and cackling maniacally. Naomi sat silently in the backseat. Mollie was relieved that she and Naomi could spend the rest of Friday alone.

Saturday morning the out-of-towners met at the motel's tacky pool. The last of the Levines, cousin Max and his wife, Gloria, had arrived from New York late the night before. Retelling the previous day's events for Gloria and Max's benefit, the Levines constructed arguments and commentary in near-Talmudic fashion. Everyone had at least one opinion about Cousin Nancy's bawdy joke. Robbie was sure it was just Southern weirdness; Sarah was convinced Cousin Nancy was trying to be hip. Mollie thought it was the punch. Naomi, usually willing to argue any side of any question just for the pleasure of argument, had nothing to say.

Then the Levines discussed where the wedding was being held. The group opinion was that Michael was a good-natured schmo to go along with a church wedding in the first place. Sarah reported that she had tried talking with Michael about some other setting or at least getting a rabbi to co-officiate. But Michael's Jewish identity was pretty much nonexistent, and he really didn't care. He had said that the wedding was Laurie Ann's domain with one exception — he wanted a dinner dance after the ceremony. That request caused no end of consternation in Laurie Ann's family, but Michael had been insistent, and the groom would get his Yankee dinner dance.

Eventually that conversation wore down, and the Levines began discussing everything they had heard about the minister performing the wedding. In the second of three required prenuptial counseling sessions, the minister had tried to get Michael to consider "embracing Christ into your life," an idea that made the entire quasi-Communist Levine clan hysterical. In the third session he had tried, without success, to discuss personal finances with Michael and wifely obedience with Laurie Ann. Michael and Laurie Ann had given preacher Smyth a number of secular readings they wanted him to include in the ceremony, but he had made it clear that he would make his decision later, after "prayerful time spent on bended knee." Commentary on the preacher was rapid-fire and very funny, but Naomi sat silently, staring into space until it was time to get dressed and go to the wedding.

The church was modern: oak pews, giant glass doors, and a huge cross ("No body," Robbie said gratefully) on the wall behind the altar. Naomi was to be escorted to their pew by Laurie Ann's surly brother, Johnny; Mollie was paired with Michael's wisecracking childhood friend, Mario. "Sure ain't Jersey!" he mumbled to Mollie in his rumbly Newark accent as they made their practice run. The rehearsal finished ninety minutes before the wedding was scheduled to begin. Mollie spent that time sitting in the back pew, wishing she were somewhere else.

The ceremony was even more awful than the Levines had imagined. Not only did preacher Smyth ignore all of the couple's suggested readings, but his sermon was a twisted homily on a mistranslation of the Hebrew word *shalom*. Nodding sanctimoniously at the groom's family, the Reverend Smyth rambled on about how "the Jewish word *shalom* means a good fit, like gears fitting together. So too should man and wife fit together like gears..." Stunned by the preacher's stupidity, Mollie looked at Naomi and her family. Robbie was twisting his mustache furiously. Sarah was staring, unseeing, in the general direction of the minister and happy couple. Naomi was sitting dead still, hands clenched in her lap. When she wouldn't even acknowledge Mollie's attempt to catch her eye, Mollie knew that Naomi was fighting to keep control.

In an effort not to stand up and yell, "'Peace,' *shalom* means 'peace,' damn it," Mollie tried to calculate how many people were at the wedding and what percent were there for the groom. The bride had far too many family and friends to maintain a bride's side; they nearly filled the church. Everyone from the groom's side fit into two short rows.

That means eighteen rows of Laurie Ann's, about... Mollie craned her neck surreptitiously. *Fifteen people in each row...* Her concentration was wavering. *Uh, 225 and forty-five, 270 for the bride, twelve for the groom.*

Finally the Reverend Smyth was finished. Laurie Ann's college friends Bobbie Sue and Monica sang "We've Only Just Begun" as the out-of-tune recessional while the congregation exited into the late-afternoon Tennessee heat. After a seemingly endless wait, the bridal party emerged from the church, and everyone formed caravans to drive to the Apex Country Club for the reception and dinner. Mollie heard several comments about the "Yankee groom's dinner" and wished that Michael had succumbed to the blissfully short Southern tradition of cake and punch in the church.

Although the country club was not very far from the church, the trip there seemed interminable because of cousin Gloria's incessant chatter.

"Maxy, how far to the country club?" she asked in her grating squawk, ignoring the fact that her husband had never been there. "Naomi, your dad would have *plotzed* at that ceremony, wouldn't he

Max?" she continued. "So *goyisher,* and in a church no less, with a minister. Thank God, Mersh wasn't around to see this. Oy," she said, breaking off in mid breath, "I can't believe he and Fanny are both gone." Turning to Mollie, Gloria continued, "Mersh and Fanny were their parents. Wonderful people, wonderful. Mersh was Max's cousin, but they grew up more like brothers. Both gone now..." Gloria lapsed into silence but only for a moment.

Mollie tried to concentrate on the scenery instead of Gloria's piercing voice. As soon as they arrived at the one-story cinder-block building (*This is the country club?* Mollie wondered), she and Naomi managed to slip away.

As they wandered aimlessly through the poolside reception, Mollie stopped smiling at guests whose smiles dropped as she and Naomi drew near. They found Robbie off the main lobby; he was preoccupied with his best man's toast. Gloria was standing dangerously near the pool edge, chattering away, although no one was standing near her. Sarah was nowhere to be found. Mollie spotted Ruthie trying to get the bartender to give her some champagne. Naomi, still smiling stiffly, was muttering about whether or not this club was "restricted." Finally it was time to be seated for dinner.

The entire Levine family didn't even fill one table. Smiling feebly at each other, Naomi and her cousins made small talk about the weather, the size of Apex, and how peculiar that Southerners thought this kind of dinner dance was odd and Yankee.

"Yankee?" Gloria asked no one in particular in her loud Brooklyn voice. "They think we're Yankees? *Gevalt,* what do these people know?"

Dinner was served, eaten, and cleared, and it was time for the best man's toast. Robbie did a great job, talking about when he married into the Levine family and how warm they had been to him. He talked about meeting Laurie Ann for the first time, and then he talked, in true "I don't know what to say" wedding-toast fashion, about how he knew that everyone in that room wished the bride and groom every happiness. He even (rather daringly, Mollie thought) acknowledged that this was a multicultural marriage, blending Jew and Gentile, Yankee and Southerner. He closed with what he called the most fitting toast he knew for this occasion: *"L'chayim,* y'all!"

Eight people at one table on one side of the room laughed. Finally politeness took over the silence, and 200 uncomprehending people clapped briefly and drank their champagne. Shortly after that the band began to play. By this time Michael and Laurie Ann's friends, seated at the next table, had graduated from almost subtle looks at Mollie and Naomi to open stares and snickers. Mollie was trying to pretend that she and Naomi weren't the objects of such open hostility; she hoped Naomi hadn't noticed.

Max was dozing in his chair, and Gloria was chatting at no one, when Naomi abruptly left the table. After twenty minutes Mollie mumbled, "Excuse me," and went to find her lover. After checking the pool deck, the side yard, and even the parking lot, Mollie finally found her in the ladies' room. Happy wedding guests entered and, surprised at what they saw, stared at the sobbing woman on the couch. Mollie sat down next to Naomi and pulled Naomi into her arms. "Want to go home, sweetie?" she asked softly. "I'll take us home right now."

"I just couldn't stand any more," Naomi said, sounding almost apologetic. "These last few days have been so hard. Right now I'm sorry we ever decided to come."

Oblivious to the ladies' stares, Mollie held Naomi close, rubbing her head softly. "It's hard to share a celebration that we can never have. And people here have made it even harder."

Angry now, Mollie looked up to glare at a woman who was staring at them openmouthed.

"Never seen lesbians before?" Mollie snapped.

The woman dropped her eyes and stammered something inaudible as she left the bathroom.

"She didn't even stay to pee," Naomi noted with a wry smile. "Mollie," she continued tearfully, "I want to go back to the motel. I know we should stay, but this feels shitty. I don't want to be here."

Nodding her agreement, Mollie stood and helped Naomi up, wiping her tear-stained face. Hand in hand they walked out of the bathroom and back to the party. Naomi's swollen eyes made an obvious lie of their "must have been too much excitement, not feeling well" excuse to the bridal party, but everyone was either too polite or too indifferent to argue. As Mollie and Naomi left, the band was playing something that sounded like "Sunrise, Sunset" with a country twang.

Back at the motel, their fancy go-to-a-wedding clothes in a heap on the floor, Mollie and Naomi lay naked on the bed, arms entwined, bellies pressed gently together.

"Why can't the universe celebrate this?" Naomi asked softly. "How come everyone feels so free to hate us?"

"Sweetie, you forget how many things we are that we're not supposed to be. We're fat, we're Jews, we're dykes, we're not the least bit ladylike. And to top it all off, we're Yenkees."

Mollie's goofy Yiddish accent made Naomi smile.

"Dollink," Mollie continued in the throaty voice she used with her best bad Yiddish accent, "you vant to run avay to the big city mit me? Ve could be vicked, vicked vomen there. Nu?" Mollie pulled Naomi closer.

"I can't wait to get on that plane in the morning," Naomi murmured. "In fact, I can't wait that

long to see just how 'vicked' we can be..."
Naomi's voice trailed off as she pushed in even
closer. Although their first kiss was tentative, the
comfort of their abiding passion soon took over
until nothing in the outside world mattered to either of them.

Baby Pictures

by

Martha Clark Cummings

When Ruth first walked into the office for part-time instructors in the English department, where we both teach, I said to myself, without even noticing that it was a sexist remark, *Here is one tough broad.*

She was wearing a red-and-black dress and earrings like pewter disks. She stood in the middle of the room, hands on her hips, her fierce hairdo pointing toward the ceiling, and said, "So where am I supposed to sit?" She was joking, of course, but I could see she was not happy.

Nobody wanted to tell her that thirty-five instructors shared five desks and if none was available, it was too bad for her, so for a while no one spoke. Finally I said pretty softly, "You can have this one. I'm on my way out."

Her dark eyes blazed. Already I wanted to give her everything.

"Thanks," she said, throwing her enormous book bag down on my desk, then standing over me, waiting. "You're all gonna glare at me when I go out for a smoke, right?" she said.

"Another smoker!" Diana exclaimed, delighted, turning around from her desk in front of me.

Baby Pictures

"Thank God. Welcome. I'm Diana. We'll loiter on the sidewalk together."

"Ruth," Ruth said, then turned to me and growled, "Ruth."

"Gail," I told her.

I left the room with Becky, another teacher.

"Ooh," she whispered. "I wouldn't want to tangle with that one."

I was already planning what I would say to her the next time I saw her.

The first thing Ruth and I ever did together, besides have coffee and bagels after teaching, was go to the Museum of Modern Art. A woman tried to cut in front of us in the ticket line.

"Hey!" Ruth said. "Are we invisible or what?"

"Sorry," the woman muttered and sheepishly ducked behind.

At the top of the escalator, Ruth had an idea. "Let's play a game," she said.

"What game?"

Up to that point the only game we'd played was "Shock Your Mother." Each time we met after class, we told each other one thing we couldn't imagine telling our mothers. We were working chronologically and hadn't even gotten to high school yet. I had last told her about the time I tripped my best friend, Billy, in the stairwell at school and the awful sound his head had made hitting the slate step. No one had seen me do it, not even him, and I had never confessed.

"Let's look at the photographs," Ruth said. "And when we find one that looks like what we want from life, tell each other."

We turned the corner into the first gallery and were confronted with a large portrait of a hairy, sagging male torso.

"Ugh," she said. "Not that, right?"

I was still not sure at that point if she meant that in general or that particular old hairy one.

I took so long, walking so slowly from one gallery to the next, hesitating in front of so many photographs and then deciding against them, that Ruth began to be impatient.

"What's the matter?" she whispered. "Scared?"

I would not choose something with people in it, I decided. I did not want to give myself away that fast. Finally I paused the longest in front of two by Edward Weston, "Sand Dunes" and "Artichoke Halved." I liked the smooth, creamy ripples in one, the delicate intricacy of the other.

"Can I have two?" I asked her.

"Sure," she said. "Which two?"

I showed her. If she asked me why, I would say that I wanted my life to have texture.

She smiled. "You-ou are ob-vi-ous," she said in singsongy fashion.

"What do you mean?" I asked.

"I want one of those," Ruth said suddenly, clutching my arm. I turned toward where she was looking.

Baby Pictures

"A tractor seat?"

"No, no, what the person's got in front of that."

As she often would in the future, Ruth was breaking the rules of her own game.

Standing in front of the photograph was a dark, delicate Italian-looking woman in a black leather jacket. I sidestepped to see what she was holding. An infant.

"Not all the other stuff that goes with it, okay?" Ruth quickly informed me when she saw my expression. "Just the baby. Look at it. Don't you want one?"

"I don't know," I told her. "It's never really seemed like one of my options."

The Italian woman moved on to another photograph. I was struck by her determination to continue in spite of her motherhood. For my own mother, my brother and I had been like a ball and chain.

As we were leaving the museum, Ruth turned to me and said, "Invite me over."

"What?" I asked, afraid that my wishful thinking had made me hear her wrong.

"Invite me over to your apartment. Don't you live around here?"

I lived on 49th Street and Second Avenue. We arrived in minutes. She didn't even wait to take her coat off but walked right up to me as soon as I had closed the apartment door and placed a soft, slow kiss on my mouth.

"Obvious," she said.

Before long my midtown studio had become our spare room, and I was living in her floor-through apartment in Park Slope.

The next time Ruth and I looked at photographs was during the period that my mother was packing up and getting ready to move to Florida. One of the many evenings I went over to help her pack, Ruth stayed home to read her students' essays. The uniformed doorman tipped his hat, the fake fire flickered in the lobby fireplace, and upstairs I found my mother standing on a ladder in the hall closet, tossing items from the top shelf into a large black plastic bag. She took down a shoebox, raised the lid and peered into it, then closed it up, throwing it in with the rest of what she had decided was trash. The mirrored hallway reflected each of her gestures dozens of times.

"Wait! What's in there?" I asked. "Shoes?"

"Baby pictures," she said, disgusted, as if it were a box of mold.

"I'll take them," I told her, reaching gingerly into the bag and plucking out the box.

"Oh, Gail," she said, "how many times can you look at the same mother and babies?"

"Over and over," I told her, "if it's us."

Ruth wanted to open up the shoebox of photos as soon as I got home.

Baby Pictures

"Let's analyze them," she said, taking the box and sitting me down at the kitchen table. She cut me a slice of the cheesecake she had made to help me get over the evening with Mom. "Let's figure out your childhood."

The first picture in the box wasn't a baby picture at all but a family portrait, the four of us on horseback, stopped on a trail somewhere in the New Jersey woods. My father and his horse were in the center of the picture. He was trying to look as if he knew what he was doing, although he couldn't possibly since all of us had just started riding. My mother looked pretty but terrified. Her hands clutched the reins as if she were sure the horse was about to start galloping and she would fall off. Actually her horse was on the very edge of the trail, in the underbrush, probably munching leaves. My brother and I were trying to look happy and proud, but there were dark circles under our eyes.

After Ruth and I had plowed through the whole boxful of pictures, figuring out nothing, this horsey portrait was still the one she liked best.

"Look," she said. "Even as a little kid you were trying to get ahead."

She is proud of me for going on to get a doctorate. She looks forward to the time when I will be a tenured professor.

I took the photograph from her and looked at it again. It was true that my horse's nose extended slightly beyond the others.

The next afternoon I came back from teaching to find that she had put the picture in an old wooden frame and hung it in the narrow hallway that runs from the front door to the kitchen.

"Okay?" the Post-it note she had slapped on the wall beside it said, and then, "XOXOXO."

Three months later, at Christmastime, we left New York on a cold, damp morning, the air heavy with snow.

"Our plane is gonna crash, right?" Ruth said matter-of-factly, and we arrived in the thick, warm air of Florida. I peeled off my sweater while my mother drove us down the palm-lined highway toward her new home. I was going to have to work very hard to like a place that had been delivered in two halves on the back of a truck. It seemed truly awful that my own mother lived in such a state of impermanence, perched on a lawn, ready to be carted off again at any moment.

Sitting on the redwood deck of my mother's double-wide, listening to the sounds of my mother doing laundry, I may as well have been the child in that horseback-riding family again. I felt just as trapped, just as melancholy. I remembered perfectly crouching on the lawn while my mother hung the laundry on the carousel in the backyard. I studied the clover and waited. If someone had asked me, I wouldn't have been able to say for what. Was I waiting to grow up? For school to start

again? I don't think so. I think I was waiting for
my mother to need me. She never did, though.
Even after my father died, she did just fine.

On the redwood deck in Tampa, I knew what I
was waiting for. Ruth had gone to Sarasota to visit
her brother's family first — to get it over with, she
said, although I know she adores them. Right then,
at least, I knew I was waiting for Ruth.

My mother came out of the laundry room holding up my bra in both hands.

"See this?" she said.

I tried to anticipate what advice or observation
she was going to offer, but I couldn't imagine.

"It's mine," she said. "It's just like yours."

"No!" I wanted to shout at her. "No, it isn't!"

But she was right. They were exactly the same.

On the day that Ruth was due to arrive, I was so
eager to see her that after waiting on the deck, listening for her rented car all morning, suddenly I
could stand it no longer. The beach was too far, so
I put on my bathing suit and went to the pool to
splash around with the old people. When I arrived
back at the house, wrapped in a towel, the two of
them were sitting at the dining room table, my
mother using Ruth's arrival as an excuse to have a
drink. Ruth was having a glass of iced coffee.

"Gail," Ruth said to me, squeezing my hand.
When her expression is serious, her large dark eyes
are especially beautiful. Sometimes I accuse her of

making them beautiful, just to see me swoon in public. She says she doesn't have that much power.

"I missed you," she said.

Ruth is not at all embarrassed in front of my mother. She thinks it's fine we're in love. Why shouldn't Mother? She even calls her that — Mother.

"They're so cute," Ruth said of her brother's children. "Joshua is six, and Esther is four, and they both love their aunt Ruth more than anyone in the whole wide world."

"Consider yourself lucky you won't be having any," my mother said bitterly.

I could feel the muscles in the back of my neck starting to knot up. This was the one subject I could actually imagine Ruth and my mother fighting over. What my mother doesn't know is this: If there's one thing Ruth regrets about this whole business of loving another woman, it's that we can't have each other's children. Sometimes we pretend we can and try to decide what they would look like and who would actually give birth. We decide that they would be dark because Ruth is — and dark is dominant genetically — and that she would get to have them because she's younger and more maternal. Then she pretends to worry that I wouldn't want to bring them up Jewish.

"Come on, Mother," Ruth said, getting up to put the gifts she has brought under the tree, "you can't tell me you didn't like having kids."

Baby Pictures

"I hated it," my mother said. "I couldn't wait until they grew up."

Ruth and I exchanged looks. Hers said, *Is she drunk or what?* Mine was more like, *I told you so.*

"But Mother," she persisted. "When they wake up in the morning with their little nightgowns on? And they're still all warm and smell so sweet?" My mother was shaking her head. "And they're so soft. When you run your hand over their soft little legs?"

"Children were like a wedge between us," my mother said, meaning her and my father.

"Don't listen to this," Ruth said to me, holding her hands over my ears. "I can't believe this. You go take a shower. I'm going to keep working on her."

In the shower I remembered one time when I was walking up Broadway toward 120th Street. I passed a woman dressed in jeans, walking slowly but not without purpose, carrying an infant on her hip, another child walking along slightly ahead of her. Suddenly the mother stopped and leaned down low toward the sidewalk, as if she had just spotted something very valuable. A twenty-dollar bill? A diamond ring? I hesitated, like the little girl, who turned to face her mother, a quizzical expression on her face, not bored, not anxious, just curious about the delay. The mother was slowly bending over, reaching for an old, almost smoked-up marijuana joint, wedged between two protrusions of a manhole cover.

"Come on, Mommy," the little girl said.

"You wait," said the mother. "Just you wait."

As she straightened up again, the baby's head flopped back, and it began to cry.

When I got out of the shower, I was relieved to find them talking about knitting. "Okay," Ruth was saying, "you're on. I'll buy the yarn and the pattern, and you'll promise not to yell at me if I'm not perfect at it the first time I try."

The next day I persuaded Ruth to go out in a canoe with me on Tarpon Lake. We put on the orange life jackets the rental company insisted that we wear. Ruth could barely close hers.

"This is ridiculous," she told the man in charge.

"That's not what I'd call it, baby," he said.

Ruth reared back, ferocious and certain as the first day I saw her, and hollered, "One more word outta you, motherfucker, and you're not gonna have any eyes to look with."

The man held his hands in the air, as if we were arresting him.

"You're from New York, right?" he said.

"Yeah," Ruth said. "Right."

Once we were in the canoe, Ruth carried on about tipping over. I put her in the bow and offered to paddle her around the lake if she would just keep still and give up on trying to steady the canoe. She reclined, facing me, and lit a cigarette. Since it was two days before Christmas, she asked me to tell her Bible stories. She did this partly to humor me. She knows how much I love to talk about God. It was the first big secret I told her, harder to reveal than any of my sexual secrets. She didn't laugh at me. Atheists have no imagination, she said.

I began with the story of Elizabeth, paddling hard as I spoke. Bible stories get my blood going. I told her all about how Elizabeth's husband, Zachariah, loses his voice for asking God too many questions.

"I love it!" she said.

And how Elizabeth can feel the baby jumping inside her as soon as Mary speaks to her.

"Wow!" Ruth said, patting the water with her flattened palms. "Then what?"

Then, I told her, they say these famous things to each other.

"Not famous for me, honey," Ruth said as a reminder.

I told her I was sure she had heard it, though. "Blessed are you among women and blessed the fruit of your womb." She hadn't.

We were in the middle of the lake. Ruth inched her way along the bottom of the canoe until she could reach my knee. She did not dare go farther, for fear of making the canoe tip over backward, she said.

"Blessed are you among women," she whispered, kissing my leg. "Is that too sacrilegious?"

"It's okay," I told her, stroking her head.

"Don't drop the paddle!" she shrieked. "Do they float?"

"Of course they do. Tomorrow I'll tell you about the trip to Bethlehem."

"That part I've heard about," she said.

That night my mother and I sat down at the kitchen table, waiting for Ruth to serve us. There had never been any question that Ruth would do the cooking. At home the kitchen is hers. I wash the dishes and shop for what she tells me to. Sometimes I ask her if she doesn't want me to cook, but she says it's okay as long as I never try to stop her from filling up the apartment with people and feeding them.

Later, while my mother and I were doing the dishes, Ruth plugged in the lights of my mother's artificial tree and poured herself a large snifter of brandy.

"I'm really getting into this," she said.

She asked my mother if she had any photo albums she could look at. My mother wiped the suds from her hands and went to look in the dresser in her bedroom. She emerged from the bedroom saying she had a surprise for us. She brought out a pink padded photo album that said ALL HER LIFE on the cover and sat down on the sofa between us. It was a book of pictures of me.

"You see," she said to me, "I didn't throw them all away."

Baby Pictures

Ruth flipped to the front of the book as if she expected to find the key to a mystery. But there was evidence of nothing. Only that I was born and began to grow, that I had a first tooth, took first steps, said a first word — a mispronunciation of my brother's name — and went to school. There was no sign of great sorrow. There was no proof of special unhappiness.

"What's the matter?" my mother asked, somehow sensing our disappointment. "What were you expecting?"

"I don't know," Ruth said, hesitating. "Something different."

In bed, in the middle of our review of the day, Ruth suddenly sat up.

"I think we should move on," she said.

"What do you mean?"

"I think we should stop looking at old photographs and go on with our lives."

"Aren't we already doing that?"

Ruth got very close to me and very still.

"Let's have a baby," she said. "Really. Let's have two. Let's go to one of those banks and make two withdrawals and get pregnant at the same time and have two babies. Okay?"

"Oh, Ruth." I put my arms around her, knowing that on some level she really meant it.

"Don't you want to?" she said. "I'm serious. Then we'll have something real to look at. Something that moves around." She gripped my shoulders. "Please?"

"Let me think about it, okay?"

It was hard to imagine. The two of us with our big stomachs squeezing past each other in the narrow hallway, and then there would be four of us...

"What would we do for money?" I asked her.

"What do we do now?" she said. "We'd keep teaching. I'd stay home and take care of the kids in the morning. You'd have them in the afternoon. On weekends we'd strap them to our backs and go to museums. Just like everyone else."

Ruth reached for a cigarette.

"I'd give up smoking for this," she said. Then she thought for a moment. "I'm going to make a pronouncement, okay?"

This meant she was serious. I nodded.

"You don't want us to have children not because we're two women and two women aren't supposed to do that together but because you're afraid you'll start acting like your mother and I'll stop loving you."

"I am not afraid," I said. "I'd never act like her."

"Prove it," she said.

"How did you get so wise all of a sudden, anyway?" I asked her, embarrassed, thinking maybe she was right.

"From hanging out with you," she said. She turned off the light. "Promise me you'll at least consider it."

Baby Pictures

"Okay," I told her. "I promise."

As I was falling asleep, I thought I heard her say that we would take them horseback riding and teach them Bible stories, but I was aware that I might be dreaming.

In Limbo

by

Deborah Schwartz

In the middle of nothing, among 200 or so bored, sleepy, good citizens of Greater Boston — heads out windows, eyes closed to shut newspapers, hands on laps or fiddling with hair, minds closed or opened to each other, families, world events — we are all waiting together in Room 216 of the Suffolk County Superior Court Room to get impaneled for jury duty or not.

Me, I like this waiting since it echoes the waiting I am doing on my heart.

My mind keeps flipping to you, then to the ocean that I swam in as a girl, then to you, then to how I need some coffee.

If they would serve us all cappuccinos and scones with butter for being such good citizens, who are trying to, being forced to, participate in the making of democracy, it would make everyone cheerier, friendlier, and certainly more acute for our jury duty, when and if the time comes.

Then to you — I remember when we first started sleeping together and my period got regular and I was crying all the time, not sure what to do with so much good sex. You said that you didn't think it was the sex but rather the amount of espresso I

In Limbo

was drinking. When we got into our first huge screaming fight, you went into my kitchen and, seeing the huge espresso pot for eleven brewing on my stove, pried open the new can of Bustelo sitting in the pantry cabinet and poured the dark, rich-like-the-earth grinds all over the kitchen floor. It was true I was drinking those eleven cups of espresso a day because I was hysterical with love and sex and caffeine, and now with these waiting citizens I remember that.

I'm thinking of you and espresso, which you've nicknamed "distresso."

I'm thinking of you swimming in the water when we lived by the ocean for a year and fought like cats and dogs but loved with our hearts wide open and greedy — you with the olive skin, you with the perfect triangular breasts, you with the short, wide legs and awkward hunchbacked bear walk. And then to the leaving of you and the memory of my mother, who beat me as a child with a rage unmatched by even the Yiddish language, only coming to its fullness when the china dishes would fall, the pot lids would tumble, and her hand would leave its red mark on my shoulder, thigh, or just-forming breasts.

Then I turn away from thinking of you into the huge, still recesses of myself. I could be leaving you because of the way I've made you into my mother, who still calls three times a week to check in on me, so she says, but really calls 'cause she thinks she needs my swollen ear to talk to or she'll die of loneliness.

I wonder though, really, has anyone ever really died of loneliness?

Maybe I'm leaving you because I love you so hard, it cracks everything open, gives me headaches, then leaves me to disintegrate into air. Or I could be leaving you 'cause during these nine ripe, lovely years, hiking with such stamina through the valley of life and death, I have grown tired.

Maybe I'm leaving you to move closer to who is the real you or, better yet, who is the real me.

Or I could be leaving you because you have said that you don't want to be pushed to change and that I am constantly pushing you to change just to keep up.

Then you would be leaving me.

Because it's true. I am changing.

I am a moth, a city pigeon — fluorescent green and purple around the eyes, a monarch butterfly with one black stripe like a racing car, anything with wings.

I am changing whether I like it or not. Often I hate it, would rather get hit by a city bus than feel the pain of this changing and the unknowingness of where it will carry me.

But instead fall comes with her warm rain.

Everything smells like attics while the leaves turn plum-red like fruit or fire, to later fall, getting caught on my jacket collar.

In Limbo

I see change looking me in my face while its own face is holy and glowing.

I am sitting here in the middle of all these waiting people, all of us on hard wooden chairs, when what I want is to be with you.

No, what I want is to be inside of you, to be swallowed up by you, to be later spit up new, whole, good.

I am trying to wait with all these waiting people, to sit still enough to seek shelter in my own cave of being, however dusty and full of bats it is. But the woman next to me, who has also been here waiting for three-and-one-half hours, has shared her *New York Times* with me, and I see in the Arts section, like the leaves landing on the ground, the words of poems old and new that have been posted on the walls of New York subways next to cigarette ads.

I want to fly to New York for the weekend to be part of the waiting, ugly, mournful crowds who, dimly lit, ride the rotten subway cars; García Lorca's words hovering over them: "Still waters of your mouth under a thicket of kisses"; Bishop's words, like tiny mirrors in the marketplace — words about the boat sinking while the boy, who stands on the burning deck, is trying to recite about the love of a boy who stands on a burning deck while that boat too is sinking.

While I am writing about you, who I am in love with and trying to leave and trying to rid you and still have you live in my red-plum heart — you who are all the things in Bishop's poems...the ship, the boy (the flames that will burn the ship and drown its passengers), the fire, you who are all these things — except the poet — out of nowhere, you appear in my row of hardware chairs.

You wake the woman who lent me the *Times*. You are wearing your blue work shirt, holding a cup of coffee and a cream-filled doughnut, which you don't intend to share.

You smile and say, "Hey," interrupting Bishop's poem and the story I am trying to write about waiting. You bring plot, conflict, desire to the scene. You are small, casual, tasty like a shelled almond.

You say, "Hey," and I light up. You are working in the courthouse, testing the air quality of the building as workers have been reporting itchy eyes and throats, dizziness, and nausea. I know that you and your environmental engineering job will fix all that, and I am so happy to see you and also happy to be writing a story about waiting.

I tell you the title of my new story, and you giggle, knowing it's about us and my heart and also about waiting with all these tired people.

I love that you understand life's paradoxes well enough to not need an explanation of the story line, which I couldn't give you anyway.

I love that when you giggle, you reveal your wide, sharp teeth and your long neck.

In Limbo

It is you I love — you who have little hands and a big heart that you constantly wrap up deep in your chest cavity. It is this life I love.

You have no words.

Life has more words than could fit in all of the skyscrapers and subway cars of New York City.

Now that you are here, I would like to collect all the poets' words on love and get some new ideas. For we two are trains passing in the night — passing, touching, passing.

But you are so smart in the eyes of life that you laugh hard when I tell you the name of the story I am writing, though you know it is about us.

You promise to buy me a Greek salad for lunch since you're pretty certain that they give us all a break at 1 P.M.

You leave with my money, telling me to come visit you for Greek salads. You tell me to come visit you in your makeshift office, which is through the elevators and up to the eighth floor, then down through some concrete steps that are behind the doors that say DO NOT OPEN EXCEPT FOR FIRE. Those doors lead you to floor 7M, then you turn left into a huge dark room filled with pipes, where your office is hiding at the back, and though it's hard to find, you will have music playing from the radio so I can hear where you are.

You tell me to come visit you at 1 o'clock, in an hour, when I imagine I will know if I've been impaneled to sit for a trial or am free to go home. Or maybe they, the judges, having not decided either way, will ask us to sit and wait longer. And this would be fine, this exercise in buoyancy, floating, a pause before the dive underwater or the slow walk back to shore.

The Birthday Party
by
Uncumber

I am pleased that no one recognizes the sea-green
silk dress that I bought last year at Secondhand
Rose. I bought it so I would look like everyone
else at the luncheon I gave, with my sister-in-law
Deirdra, for my niece who was getting married.

Every time I go back home for an event, I ex-
amine my clothes and decide whether I must go
buy something for the occasion. Years ago I acquired a white-and-brown two-piece dress at Nei-
man Marcus in Dallas. I used it many times for
family gatherings, hoping that no one would remember it from the year, or years, before. Finally
that dress was no longer a classic that could go
anywhere, any season, because fashion had moved
so far that even classics were left behind. I had to
search for another dress.

There was a moment in the shop, when the clerk
held the rippling silk against the faintly amber skin
of her cheek and her golden hair drifted forward
against the fabric, that I thought of Louise. The
aqua-green dress would have been perfect for her.
It was fine for the luncheon.

I never once slipped when complimented. I did
not say, "Oh, thanks. I found it at a secondhand

shop. Isn't it great? It was probably worn only a couple of times."

Now here I am, wearing this lovely dress again a year later at Ned's sixtieth birthday party. It seems strange having a younger brother who is sixty years old. I'm beginning to understand how my grandmother felt. Looking in the mirror, she wondered, *Who is that old lady?* She said she felt like eighteen or twenty and never got over the shock of looking at her reflection and seeing the "old lady" looking back at her.

When I took the dress from the closet to pack for this celebration trip, I thought of Louise again. Yes, this dress is her color, but it looks okay on me too. I took the dress from the hanger, folded it carefully with layers of tissue paper tucked in the folds to prevent wrinkling — as I had been carefully taught to do at that finishing school politely called a college — and I wondered if Louise would be at my brother's party. If she were, then her husband, Harold, would be there too. *There will be dancing,* I had mused as I pressed down the lid of the suitcase, *and Harold can't keep off her feet. He always steps on her. What a klutz.*

Oh, how she and I had danced, evenings and afternoons in the living room of her mother's house. Very young. Our bodies were born to dance together. We had another language. When we danced — close — our bodies spoke with one voice.

The Birthday Party

Would she be glad to see me? How would I feel facing her in the gathering of couples, alone? My lover was not coming along. My family still clung to their picture of me as one of the many older women who mistakenly allowed her marriage of many years to drift on the rocks and who was now doomed to spend the rest of her life lonely, with no man to look after her or, most important, to take her on trips, to dinner, to the theater. They were not yet ready, I told myself, to know that I had chosen a new life, a new love after a half century of denying my gay reality.

I had never been less lonely than now, and I had never been happier. But in the midst of the crowd, the noise, the music, would I be seized with a deep nostalgia, a pain that I detest yet can't entirely escape, especially when I am in that country among those old friends and relatives. Especially if Louise is present. Every person encounters places, sounds, and smells that touch the strings of the harp carried since adolescence and make them vibrate. And if the first love was one denied — not allowed to run its instructive course — then the nostalgia is particularly deep, sentimental, and dangerous. These vibrations resonate with tragic love stories and explain, in part, our fascination with renunciation and unrequited love.

Did I deserve such a perfect sister-in-law? Deirdra had been organizing this party for almost an entire year. It is a huge surprise party, and it is

obviously a huge success. There are over 200 of
Ned's friends here and all of his children and their
children. Deirdra managed to keep this gathering a
secret, but I don't know how. Ned was definitely
stunned when he walked in. No one gave it away,
not even the young children — my beautiful great-
nieces and -nephews.

I watch several of them dancing to the music of
the small jazz band that Deirdra has hired. They
mix with the adults on the dance floor, who smile
down at them and move aside to give them room.
Elizabeth and Anne — cousins, nearly four years
old, one blond and the other with dark curls —
absorbed in each other and the music, dancin' and
stompin' to the fine jazz. I love it. I am home. And
they are young, and they are cousins. It doesn't
matter if everyone else in the dance is matched
boy-girl, man-woman.

I catch my Uncle Jerome's eye as he taps his toe
and snaps his fingers. We step out with the beat.
He is a great dancer, and we fly around the floor,
clearly delighting our younger kin.

Uncle Jerome's wife, Melony, is sitting at a
table on the edge of the dance floor. Who is that
with her? Louise? Yes, and Harold. I didn't notice
them entering. There is such a crowd — so many
people I haven't seen in such a long time — so
much noise. The three are drinking white wine
and nodding the polite way of people just getting
acquainted.

The Birthday Party

Uncle Jerome and I leave the floor and make our way in their direction. The music begins again. My chest is tight, and the tears start to gather in my eyes. There she is, Louise, my first love, my first lover. All the reasons she and I never speak of this, all the reasons I left home and live thousands of miles away and carefully reveal only a small part of my life to these kin and friends who urge me to move back home but who could never take me back, not the real me, rise up. The reasons bring feelings that press and spread out inside me.

The rhythm deepens. The clarinet sings and screeches. I will dance with her. I will ask her, and she will say yes. People may stare, but we will dance. There may be questions too and awkward words with my brother, but that will be later. I will dance with her. I will have one more time after all these years, one more time around the floor, this jazzy floor with her.

I lean close. I ask her. She takes my hand that I place near hers on the table.

In the Heat of the Moment
by
Roey Thorpe

It proved to be one of the most disastrous deci-
sions I've ever made, but there, in the heat of the
moment, it was right, oh, lord, was it right! It
made a train wreck of my life, but looking back,
I'd do it again. Hell, I'd do it twice.

I mean, me, a quasi-Jewish girl, on the fat end of
fat, a good girl always, albeit with some fairly
controversial politics, having sex in the hallway of
my apartment building (we didn't even make it inside, that's how hot it was, how dangerous) with
her, also Jewish, but never good. She was bad, she
was terrible, maybe even evil as it turned out, and
there we were, her with one hand wound in my
long curly hair, pulling my head back to expose
my throat, which she was biting — gnawing on,
even — ah, vampire, if this is immortality, I'll take
it, bring it on, hurry up!

Her other hand was shoved inside my panties,
palm up, and me, I was just hanging on, my nails
putting half-moon scars on her leather jacket, intoxicated by the residue of the 10,000 joints
smoked by its wearers, including the crack addict
she had stolen it from late at night as he lay passed
out in a New York City subway station. I had only

read about someone this tough before, someone who would *be* in a New York City subway after dark, much less steal something in one — God, the fantasy of it all! I grabbed on tighter and buried my face deeper in that smoky jacket and wished I had the nerve to utter some completely lurid phrase but was afraid I'd blow it, so I just gasped and sighed and tried to make my bosom heave like it would in the romance novels where I'd read about encounters like this with people like her, and it wasn't hard to heave under the circumstances, really.

And later, much later, as my life seemed impossible and as I realized how truly afraid of this woman I had become, I tried to find regret for that first hallway encounter, tried to pin it as the first hairline crack in my shattered life but just couldn't say I was sorry, that it wasn't worth it, because it was, it certainly, certainly was.

Teacher

by
Yvonne Fisher

She was my teacher. I noticed her. She taught me many things. She was the director of my theater group. She had a quiet voice. She taught us that theater was about our lives. We had something to say. She let us say it. She was slow. We did yoga. She trained our voices. She had black hair. She did experimental theater. She made us go deep. She had a gentle touch. She knew so much. I admired her. I learned from her.

We walked home together. She had a bicycle. I was in a relationship. She was my teacher. Something happened. We didn't know. She was quiet inside. She taught mè many things.

We did a three-act musical. We did improvisations. It was very exciting. We went further and further. We didn't know. We tested the boundaries. The theater group was there. We went out for a drink. We talked about theater. I played a painter. It was Romaine Brooks. There was Natalie Barney. This was our play. It was lesbians in Paris. It was turn-of-the-century. There was Dolly Wilde, the niece of Oscar. There was Renée Vivien, the anorexic poet. It took years to develop. We read books about them. We wrote songs

Teacher

about them. We took singing lessons. None of us could sing.

She was the director. We followed her lead. We got a choreographer. We learned to dance. We went out on a limb. She taught us well. We couldn't turn back. The theater work excited us. She was my teacher. She had things I wanted. There was something in her voice. There was something in her touch. There was something in her eyes. Something kept us going. The theater work excited us.

We went out for a drink. She had her bicycle. Natalie and Romaine. It was like this. This was how it started. It was this simple. We walked home together. She had her bicycle. I was in a relationship. Natalie and Romaine. Ménage à trois. Paris, 1920. American expatriates. No turning back. We walked into her building. We went into the elevator. It started moving up. The lights were low. The theater work was deep. We were standing in the elevator. Something happened. We didn't know. I held my breath. We were learning so much.

We went out for a drink. We touched under the table. The theater work was deep. I held my breath. I couldn't breathe. She was my teacher. Director of my theater group. I was in a relationship. So mixed-up. Natalie and Romaine. Dolly Wilde. Liane de Pougy. Famous courtesan. Rich lesbians. Artists' salons. Do you see how it happened? It was so illicit. We were standing in the elevator. There was no turning back. I was in Paris. We were singing songs. We waltzed around the room. Her hair was black. The moon was full.

Later we read books together. Later we dressed up. Later we liked the same things. Later we laughed a lot. Later we talked about it all. Later my neck got stiff. Later we couldn't get it right. Later we misunderstood. Later I couldn't turn my head. My neck was stiff. We couldn't get it right. Later we didn't know where to turn. I was so mixed-up.

We went to the reservoir. We sat in the car. We tried to part. She went one way. I went another. We tried to make peace. We tried to understand. Later she threw the glass against the wall. The glass shattered. The blood was dripping. I held my breath. I couldn't breathe. The glass was shattered.

Nothing was the same. We had differences. It interfered with the work. It made the work richer. We stayed in our roles. She was my teacher. It hurt us so much. We tried to part. Like strangers on a train. We didn't understand. The work became beautiful. The glass had shattered. Blood against the wall. Everybody gasped. Nothing under the table. Couldn't turn my neck. Nothing looked right. Nothing tasted good. Nothing made sense. Except the shatter on the wall. The blood was dripping.

We went back to our lives. Nothing was the same. The work continued. The work got richer. We used our pain. We used each other. We used ourselves. We used what we had. We had enough.

Teacher

The glass against the wall. The death of our passion. We sat in the car. The reservoir was there. She didn't want to do it. The rain was coming down. Crash against the glass. The rain was coming hard. We didn't want to know. It never made much sense. It had a life of its own.

The theater work was good. We didn't know how to do it. We tried every way. Nothing was the same. The rain was shattering. The glass was filled. I threw it against the wall. Everybody gasped. The blood was coming down. I tensed my heart. My neck got stiff. There was a scream. Like someone was killed. The work got richer. This was our goal. She was my teacher.

I led the way. I didn't know where. We knew what we wanted. Life of its own. We sat in the car. We took a trip. The rain was pouring down. We both were cold. I needed another blanket. The glass was shattered. Natalie and Romaine. Paris, 1920. No turning back. We tried every way. We couldn't find a way. We wanted it to work. The work got richer. We couldn't forget. We couldn't let go. We couldn't go on. We couldn't stop. We didn't know. We kept on working. We played our parts. We were characters in a play. We sang, and we danced.

She was my teacher. She taught me many things.

Amour, Amour

by
Maureen Brady

I. First Kiss

We walk the river park, gazing out, then back at each other, our eyes sparkling with blue, yours more like the water, glinting green. I want to hold your hand but hardly know you. Hardly know how to say why my heart keeps wanting to home in next to yours.

Your hands are busy, possibly nervous. You tell me how you embarked to see the world in youth, your European travels. The couple you stayed with in Germany who made love in front of you. I see your innocence standing side by side with your determination to escape the provinces you grew up in and become worldly. Remember my own rickety shuttle through youth: The man on the train who reached for my crotch behind the screen of his *New York Times,* the photographer who wanted to shoot a toothpaste commercial of my smile but said I'd need to expose my breasts as part of the audition. *People do things like this,* I thought but did not say, that same determination overriding my dismay.

The mention of sex from your lips makes me study them all the harder, and this only makes me want to hold your hand again. We are sitting on a step by then. I lean into your shoulder, press it for a second. You say you are moving to the other step because you need to smoke a cigarette, if I don't mind. I don't. I want to smoke myself again for the first time in over a decade, watching your small ritual — your fingers holding the cigarette, your breath imbibing it, the smoke curling upward. I wonder if I am going to get myself in trouble if I draw up the courage to kiss you.

You more or less ask how lesbians decide to kiss each other, confessing that you've nearly always been with men. I relate my coming-out, the agony of the days I waited for the woman to seduce me before I realized she was patiently, respectfully awaiting me, since I'd declared myself straight.

All the way back up beside the river, I think about your hand, how nice it would be in mine, how awkward it feels to keep apart like friends, like strangers, like birds flitting from branch to branch but landing beside each other.

Later, after you feed me the delicious pasta sauce you've stirred all day, making it into an aphrodisiac, I bump your shoulder again, this time with my head, as if I am a lowing sheep, and you grab it with your arm and hold it for a moment. Then, before thought can come again, I hold your hand, and you hold mine, and who can say who made that happen. It doesn't matter. It makes me bold enough to lean across and kiss you.

Some days down the line, you say, "You can tell if someone will be a good lover by the way they kiss, don't you think?"

"I could tell about you," I say, remembering your desire, how it captured my upper lip and pulled at me and made me want to go into your tide, utterly.

II. Possession

I think I am too tired to come. Maybe too tired to have sex. But then I think I'll let you do what you want to anyway. And you go exploring with your fingers. You rub my clit, which seems almost indifferent for a short time, though for all the past days our sex has never been ordinary.

You work at it. You don't give up. And then you go with your mouth licking me, and somewhere in there I feel your energy come into focus. Your power becomes the shape of a cone, as if you are a tornado touching down and I am the earth you want to ruffle.

My head falls back farther, my limbs go slack, my cunt goes open. You come back up and hold me, one arm surrounding me as if I were a baby. You lift me onto your leg and fuck me with your other hand and watch me swoon and come to you. And come some more. Circling high into the sky. Leaving this planet for the moment. Yet never leaving you behind. You take me everywhere I go. You take me.

Amour, Amour

III. Separation

You disappeared. How could you disappear so utterly when I thought you were right behind me. It's what I fear the worst, the most — complete desertion and disappearance. You told me we were close to danger, that I should back up. I thought you meant retrace our steps to the other subway line. I thought you were right behind me. I went single-mindedly, my head never turning around, trusting you were in my footsteps. When I turned around you were nowhere. There was blank air. There were strangers. There was silence and frigid air.

I was lonely right away like I'd been before I met you. Before you arrived in my life looking wholesome, possible, eager, lovely.

My heart fell down an elevator shaft into a bottomless hole. There was no landing. I peered at all the people, called your name, not out loud, which would make me seem crazy since you were not there, but silently I prayed your name. Retraced my steps, searching as one examines the weave of a fabric for a misstitch. How could the weave come apart when it had been coming together so exquisitely. When your head lying upon my shoulder had come to feel placed there by an angel. When your popping an apple slice into my mouth had come to be an anointing.

You have been gone one day and one night, and this is what I dream.

Maureen Brady

IV. Reunion

You fly home in bad weather. I don't want you flying in an ice storm, but I don't want you to be late either. I've borne our days apart with whole segments of me submerged in a holding tank, and I don't know if I can bear another.

We undress each other slowly. Our bare chests touch tenderly, our breasts get kissed and greeted. My eyes search your face, roam your body, learning you all over again, while recruiting memory of the routes that have become familiar.

A pitch of fear mediated by desire into a high, thin note hangs in the air, vibrating. We dart from our memories of separation to our memories of union. We are new again, and yet your smell has gained a hold on me with ancient remnants to it. I fall headlong into your spell. Your mouth is so soft, I am amazed once more at the power it has to flood me.

Length to length, our pants kicked off, our hearts joined, our mounds shimmer a current from one to the other and back again. We create a sensation that both anticipates and quite possibly surpasses the pleasure of orgasm. I say, "Can I die now? Because I think I've gone to heaven."

And you say, "No, I want you right here, on earth," and know you have me.

I lick you until enough light teems out of you to adorn the crown of my head, which makes me

Amour, Amour

wonder how sex ever got associated with badness,
when it is good enough to tell us we are home.

In Case of Emergency

by

Anndee Hochman

We buried Hank's umbilical stump in the backyard, in sight of the basketball hoop, spitting distance from where the cucumbers will be. Emmy
donated the box from her first pair of real earrings,
and we nestled the stump on the little mattress of
cotton. It was about as big as my thumb.

Hank's mother, Della, who was certifiably nuts
but had moments of stunning lucidity, sent us the
remains of Hank's umbilical after her last visit.
His dementia was pretty advanced by then, and
Hank kept calling her "Morning Glory," which
was actually his own drag name, but we didn't tell
her that.

Two days after Della got on the bus for Newark,
a small envelope arrived via Federal Express. Inside was a Ziploc bag, and inside that was the des-
iccated leftover of the cord that, thirty-four years
earlier, had looped Della and Hank together in a
perfect ecosystem. Obviously Della was cutting
her ties, shedding the apron strings and the apron
too. That package said, "He's your responsibility
now." As if we didn't know.

At first I thought it was a piece of dried-up cat
poop. But Mo, who'd worked in a women's health

clinic, recognized the rust-brown withered bit for what it was.

"Gross," Emmy said when we told her. "I hope you two didn't save mine."

We hadn't, actually — even though placenta rituals were coming back in vogue when we gave birth to Em. Some of our friends even cooked theirs into soup. That sounded revolting, so we'd wrapped ours in the Sunday comics and buried it in the yard.

It was getting crowded out there. Already underground were Moishe the hamster, Hemingway the parrot, Nora the goldfish, a stray cat that died before we'd had time to name her, and Mo's diaphragm, which she'd given a ritualistic burial to mark her coming-out years ago. It was an ethical dilemma at the time, diaphragms not being biodegradable, but Mo finally justified the burial by thinking of all the condoms, spermicide tubes, and K-Y she'd have used if she'd stayed straight. Surely her diaphragm was a lesser contribution to the nation's landfill.

Hank wanted to be buried in the yard too ("I need to apologize to Moishe for saying his tail was ugly," he said), but it turned out the county had laws about the disposal of bodies on private property, and it's hard to find the chutzpah for civil disobedience when you can't stop crying. So we had him cremated and threw the ashes off Steel Pier in Atlantic City, which was his second choice. The gray crumbs floated for a moment, then a wave came in like a giant claw and snatched Hank into the undertow.

On the way back from the shore, we told stories. How Hank loved the sound of words and would pronounce his favorites — *unctuous, serendipity, calcification* — again and again until they sounded like gibberish. How he knew things — the difference between braise and sauté, how to knit a sock, what Molly bolts were for. How he'd come over to tune our piano one August and just stayed.

Hank collected trivia and folklore but never made you feel stupid for not knowing. He told us the slang for *gay* and *lesbian* in a dozen languages. The only ones I remember are *faygeleh* in Yiddish and *mal flores,* "bad flowers," in Spanish. Hank knew the names of the Indian tribes who lived here before, and he told us that Poe's raven, the actual bird, was stuffed and preserved and stood on a closet shelf at the central branch of Philadelphia's Free Library. All you had to do was ask.

That trip to the library was his last one out of the house. All the way there in the car, Hank and Emmy recited "The Raven" and "Annabel Lee" and any other Poe they could remember. Em's favorite line, naturally, was "Nevermore!" which she'd begun using in answer to routine questions from Mo and me: "Emmy, would you like some string beans?" "Nevermore." "Em, how about practicing the piano?" "Nevermore!"

In Case of Emergency

The two of them were giddy with adrenaline and springtime, so Mo and I pretended not to notice that Hank felt like a cheap marionette — all balsa wood and paper-clip hinges — when we lifted him from the backseat into the wheelchair. Emmy skipped along beside him, singing lines from Poe, until we got to the library closet where the raven was kept. As soon as the librarian opened the door and a smell of old bones floated out, I saw Hank's hand grip the arm of his chair. The bird's feathers were the tired black of ruined suede gloves, its eyes flat and opaque, its beak yellowed. It listed to one side as though it would rather lie down.

"Close it," Hank said to the librarian, and when her hand paused a minute on the knob, he said it again. "I mean it. Close the goddamned door."

Emmy began to cry. We drove home in silence.

Even after that Hank still had the energy for our postdinner games of Clue, all four of us crowded on his bed. He always took Miss Scarlett, of course, and made absurd guesses full of political and artistic allusion.

"Colonel North with an Uzi in the Persian Gulf room," he'd say, or "Van Gogh with a paintbrush in the atelier."

"What's an atelier?" Emmy asked, and Hank explained that Van Gogh had made himself crazy in his studio from eating lead-based paint.

"Why?" Em said, and even Hank did not have an answer to that. "Why?" she said again and greeted our silence with an impatient toss of her hair. At ten she was just discovering the depths of what grown-ups do not understand. We failed her daily, but so far she had managed to forgive our astonishing ignorance.

"Mom, could Hank be my dad?" she asked once shortly after he started to live with us.

Mo and I exchanged the "Okay, here goes" look. We were all set to explain sperm donors and insemination clinics and Moms Who Really Want a Baby, but then Mo said, "How come, sweetie?"

"I mean, I know he's our friend and our housemate and everything, but there's a father-daughter basketball dinner, and I thought maybe he could just pretend."

As it turned out Hank got sick and couldn't go, so Mo escorted Emmy to the dinner. She even wore a dress. There was a gay father who spotted Mo's drag right away, and the two of them had a great time talking. Emmy won the Player With the Best Vocabulary award. I stayed home and blotted night sweats with a Mickey Mouse beach towel.

That was last spring, a year ago. Now we are burying Hank's umbilical stump and saying what we will remember most.

"His hot-and-sour soup," said Mo, who falls asleep at night reading back issues of *Food & Wine.*

"The sound of his voice," I said.

Em shifted from one foot to the other. "What he told me about dying," she said finally. "He told me it hurt and that he didn't believe any of that stuff about white light and angels but that he wouldn't mind hanging out with other dead people because they were some of the most interesting. Except for us, that is."

She bent down and put the white box in the hole I'd dug. Mo troweled dirt over it, then wiped her face with a brown hand.

"Bye, Hank," Em said. "Nevermore."

"Never more," I said. "Never enough."

In the fall, when the ground is gray and the sun sets early, we will plant bulbs in the place where Hank's umbilical cord is buried. We will choose sultry yellow irises and black-purple tulips, crazed fiery mums and lilies that arch open without the slightest hint of prudishness. Hank's cord will turn to mineral dust and mix with the remains of Moishe and Hemingway and the nameless cat, and everyone will forgive everyone. We'll weep daily into the garden. By next spring our yard will be a ruckus of brave blooms, roots tangling underground, a whole field of *mal flores.*

Sand Slip Away
by
Pam McArthur

The rental cottage is pure Cape Cod: a gray-shingled house nestled in a sandy hollow, sheltered from the June sun by scraggly pitch pines. Rough clumps of uncut grass pock the yard, and pine needles scatter underfoot.

The weathered steps creak as we climb to the porch. We drop our suitcases in the house — Rachel in one bedroom, I in the other — and jump back into her maroon Camry for the short drive to the beach.

When we park the car and clamber over the dunes, the smell of the ocean overwhelms me. That rush of low-tide odors: drying kelp, crabs, exposed sediment filled with burrowing sea life. I breathe it in as I look across the damp sandy flats with their thick fringe of marsh grass. Then we walk down onto the beach, crunching over broken shells. Bits of mussel and moon snail, clam and slipper shells nip my feet. Below the high-tide line, the beach stretches smooth and faceless to the water.

Rachel and I snake our way to the ocean's edge, skirting brightly striped towels and umbrellas lanced into the sand. The air is thick with the shriek of the gulls and the muffled reverberation as the ocean breaks just beyond the sand flats.

Standing at the lip of the ocean, I fling my arms wide.

"This is heaven."

"You know what, Martha? I've never liked the idea of heaven."

"Huh," I grunt noncommittally. I know exactly what she wants. Even without looking up I know her dark eyes are flashing, her lithe body alight with excitement as she waits for me to respond. She thrives on argument. Loves it like an otter loves a deep, clear pool. Dives in, ripples through effortlessly, emerges sleek and shiny only to dive in again.

"Well," I drawl at last, "what is so terrible about heaven?"

"Just *think* about it. Good lord, all those generations of dead people. By now it must be as much fun as a New York subway at rush hour. Maybe friendlier but still...awfully crowded."

"Oh, no, I don't think so." I enter the fray. "Souls don't take up any room at all."

She picks up a bright green clump of seaweed, spreading its long, tuberous fingers. "Maybe your soul doesn't take up any room, Martha, but mine wants some elbow space. And think about this — we're talking about everyone who's ever lived, going way back to Cro-Magnon or whatever. Now what on earth would I have to say to one of them?"

"I'm sure you'd think of something," I say pointedly.

"And go back even further. There must have been a time when we were half ape. Are those souls in heaven?"

"We can't rule out the possibility. And, of course, that raises the question of animals."

"That's easy. Animals have more right to heaven than we do. No conscience, no guilt."

"Wait a minute." I stoop to pick up a rounded calico rock. Its warm freckles make me think of Rachel's shoulders. "Are you telling me that *all* animals go to heaven? Insects too, like cockroaches and ticks and mosquitoes?"

"You've got to admit, the idea of heaven is losing some appeal, isn't it?" She laughs wholeheartedly.

I toss my pebble into the ocean, where it disappears with a faint plink. Picking up another rock, pure white and nearly translucent, I struggle to keep up my end of the argument.

"Well, without a body, maybe mosquitoes would be all right."

"Ha! I bet all that's left when the body's gone is that horrible buzzing. And you won't have a hand to slap it away!"

I slip the white rock into the pocket of my shorts, fingering its smooth surface as I consider this predicament.

"And imagine all those souls saying, 'You squashed me when I was a bug!'"

Sand Slip Away

"So you agree, heaven doesn't sound very heavenly?" She grins, the same grin that followed me all through high school. Up and down college halls too and in and out of the doorways of cheap apartments. That grin sent me off to my first job as a fledgling computer analyst. It was my lifeline as I fell in and out of love too many times with too many women. Now we are well into our thirties; I'm settled in a condo in central Massachusetts, and she, forty miles away, is coming up for tenure at her university. But still the grin is there. Still she challenges every assumption, creating chaos so that we can put the pieces back together.

We have walked far along the curve of beach and now approach a deserted stretch of sand. The sun, riding high, welds my tank top to my back.

"Hot," I say.

"Mmm."

"So, Rachel…" my voice turns husky. "Rachel, how are you…really?"

"How am I?" She glances at me, her face with that openly smug look of a cat on a sunny windowsill. "I'm great. Really great!"

This is not what I expected. She has had a tumultuous year, working her way out of a ten-year relationship, and the last time we spoke she was full of pain and regrets.

"Oh, it's still not easy," Rachel says, reading my thoughts. "Ten years — good lord, ten years even in a bad relationship carries a lot of weight!"

Weight is the right word for it. It had hurt me to watch her sink into the sullenness of that relationship, losing herself; her penchant for argument growing a nasty edge of hostility.

"It was hard to admit that things were over," she says. "She made me feel so guilty, like I hadn't tried hard enough. But now, for the first time in years, I feel alive. That's the only word I can think of — I'm *alive*."

"I'm glad. Oh, so glad!"

Turning to face her, I see clearly the woman I have loved all these years. Her eyes gleam, her hair tangles in the wind, her skin glows in the afternoon light. She has never looked more beautiful. I take both her hands in mine, dancing the line we have drawn over the years, the line of flirtation and desire unspoken, always present, always a little dangerous. Energy whirls around us, pulling us into a breathless vortex where our lips meet. Hers are moist and salty and linger a moment. Then she drops my hands and springs across the sand, galloping into a tidal pool.

"Yow! It's cold!"

She whoops, and I laugh. Though the day is hot and heavy, it is only mid June, and the ocean has not yet been claimed by summer.

"Cold?" I call back to her. "You're only up to your ankles!"

And I charge past her, splashing as much as I can. I dash over a narrow sandbar into deeper water. The shock of the cold nearly stops my heart, but I throw myself in recklessly, throwing an unspoken challenge back to Rachel.

She responds, of course, by flinging herself into the ocean, sending a cold wash of water into my face. We roughhouse through the salty tide until finally I emerge, panting, and sink to the rough beach sand.

My tank top and shorts wrap clammy fingers around me. Sand scratches its way inside my clothes.

"Ugh," I groan. "I thought we were only going to *walk* on the beach."

"Well, don't blame me. You're the one who went flying into the water."

"But you started it."

"No way!"

"Yes, way."

I wriggle my shoulders in the sand and close my eyes against the sky's glare. Drying like driftwood in the sun, I am too lazily content to argue for long. Rachel drops to the sand beside me, and I listen to the gradual slowing of our breath. Finally I squint across the short span of sand to search her face.

"Rachel?"

"Hm?"

"There *is* a heaven. I'm living in it right now."

"Oh, no, this is just a temporarily pleasant interlude…"

Pam McArthur

Her voice rushes on like clouds on a bright, windy day, changing shape, regrouping, slipping over the horizon. Always more coming. Smiling, I study the blue haze above. I could fall into this sky, and it would catch, cradle, carry me back through all the years it has arched over Rachel and me.

At last we rise and head back. Keeping stride, we walk along the packed sand. Step forward, step forward, arms swinging as our shoulders almost touch. We are nearing the parking lot when she says, "Marty?"

The childhood nickname, spoken in her full adult voice, catches at my heart.

"I never told you what made me know finally that I had to go through with the breakup."

She pauses, for once having trouble finding words. Waiting, I watch a single gull plummet to the water. The gull rises triumphant, a fish in her sienna beak.

"You know what happened? I finally realized that I was trying to turn her into you. I kept saying, 'If only she were more like Marty. More open and smart and everything else like Marty.' If only I loved her like I love you."

I watch the sand slip away under our feet as we walk. Another hour, and the tide will turn. Soon the ocean will claim this landscape; soon we will not be able to walk here.

"Martha," she says, slipping her hand under my elbow. "What I realized is, I love you — of course,

Sand Slip Away

I've always loved you — and more. I'm attracted to you."

The beachgoers that we pass don't see her fingers stroking the inner skin of my arm. They don't see the electricity crackling between us, raising the hairs at the nape of my neck and stunning the breath from my body.

"You're crazy!" I burst out.

She laughs deep in her throat. "That's what I like about you — you're so romantic."

"Well, it's true. You're crazy." We have reached her Camry, and she unlocks the passenger door. I don't get in. It is only this public space that keeps me from leaning full-bodied into her; I ache to touch her, ache all over. "Crazy," I repeat doggedly.

"Tell me why," she challenges.

"For starters, you are only just out of a long-term relationship."

"It's been months now. And it was over so long ago, it's like I've been single for years."

"It's not the same. Trust me. This is totally nuts."

Rachel unlocks the driver's door and slides onto the seat. I hesitate, then get in on my side, flattening myself against the door. Rachel slits her eyes sideways, reading my profile.

"Maybe you're right. But Marty, I had to tell you how I'm feeling."

A squat white ice-cream truck jingles into the parking lot and settles nearby. Children swarm past our car, fists closed tightly on their money, eyes eager and innocent. I am jealous of their youth. I want to be that innocent; I want to stretch eagerly for the treat offered me. I want life to be that simple.

"And I have to ask you, Marty. Ignoring the fact that I'm crazy…do you feel the same?"

I turn to meet her gaze. Searching her eyes, I reach back in memory and pull out the truth. Over the years I never let myself be conscious of my desire for her, but it was there all along, whirling at the edges of our friendship.

"Yes," I finally answer. "Yes, I feel the same."

She smiles, her face open as a sunflower in full bloom. Turning the key in the ignition, she backs out of the parking space.

"But this is still crazy!"

"I know," Rachel answers quietly. "But it's not really, because I *know* you. I'm safe with you, not afraid of losing myself. You always challenge me to be *more* myself, not less."

"That's because I love who you are."

Blood surges through my body, every nerve alive and hopeful, but I stare silently out the window. We drive through low sandy hills covered with twisted pines as well as black cherry, red maple, and alder. Soon we will reach the cottage, and I don't think I am ready.

"I'm scared," I say at last. Rachel puts her hand on my leg, a simple touch that would have brought comfort a day ago, even an hour ago. But now all

Sand Slip Away

I feel is the heat of her fingers on my skin, the first touch of true desire, the beginning of the opening of possibilities.

"We don't have to act on our feelings," I say.

"No."

"You are my best friend."

"That shouldn't be an insurmountable problem." I hear the laughter held back.

"But what if it doesn't work out? I don't want to lose you—"

"Martha." She slows the car to make the final turn, coasting to a halt in front of our cottage. "Whatever happens, you won't lose me. You couldn't get rid of me if you tried! I love you. I always will."

I turn and slip my arms around her. The contours of the car make it awkward, our first new embrace, but I am aware of every dancing atom of her flesh against cloth against my flesh. I breathe deeply at the bare, salty skin of her neck.

"Oh, God," I whisper, "I love you too."

Slowly I raise my head, brushing my cheek against hers, bringing my lips surely to the warmth of hers. If the world stopped now, if there were no other reason for life, this would be enough. This. This kiss.

But this kiss makes me reckless, and, yes, how I do want more.

"Come inside," I say to her. We move into the unfamiliar house and find our way to this room. I

Pam McArthur

look at her, this woman I love, yes, I want, yes, hunger rising as I reach openmouthed for her, open, opening.

"Is this okay?" she asks, and my bones turn to water at her tenderness.

Yes, this is, yes, and fingers creep under shirts as slow as the tide coming in and just as natural, and breasts, finally naked in their element, leap like dolphins to meet breasts like dolphins to breathe through sleek skin the air, the silver liquid air.

I never believed I could breathe underwater until now — now, when we turn slippery as fish and dive and dive and dive again to reach the secret places we have never touched. I leave my accustomed body, I turn amphibious, I breathe this woman, yes, I breathe her into my body, and this woman, yes, I love; she is familiar to me even in her naked skin and yet so new, so unexpected, and so, yes — I say yes.

When at last we leave the salt sea and I find myself naked and landlocked with this woman, it is still, yes, this woman that I love. I feel such fierce pride, and I want to shout aloud, be heard across the world. The world that could stop now and this would be enough. This.

I do not shout. Breath comes to me from ordinary air now, pulling me into a new ordinary life with her. Watching the colors shifting in the depths of her eyes, I whisper, "Now do you believe in heaven?"

Sand Slip Away

"On earth," her answer full of kisses. "Heaven on earth, yes."

From the bright circle of her arms I look up. The day is softening into dusk, the corners of the room disappearing in shadow, the air purple with the scent of pines. I think I hear through the open window the rough beat of the ocean, but perhaps it is just the wind in the trees and the steady pounding of my heart.

Contributors' Notes

Harlyn Aizley's writing has appeared in journals and anthologies including *Caffeine, Poetry Motel, Mediphors, Dialogue Magazine, Inside Magazine,* and the *Women's Studies International Forum.*

Maureen Brady is the author of *Give Me Your Good Ear, Folly,* and *The Question She Put to Herself* as well as three books of nonfiction. She lives in New York City, where she teaches writing workshops at The Writer's Voice, N.Y.U., and the Peripatetic Writing Workshop. She is completing a new novel, *Ginger's Fire.*

Cathy Cockrell is the author of *Undershirts and Other Stories* and *A Simple Fact,* both from Hanging Loose Press. "Muffie's Midnite Lounge, 1958" is part of a novel, *One of My Tribe.*

Martha Clark Cummings is the author of *Mono Lake: Stories* (Rowbarge Press). She lives in Thermopolis, Wyoming.

Yvonne Fisher is a psychotherapist, actor, and writer. She divides her time between Ithaca, New York, and New York City.

Carolyn Gage is a lesbian-feminist playwright, author, and performer. Her collection of plays, *The Second Coming of Joan of Arc and Other Plays* (HerBooks, 1994), was named a national finalist for the 1995 Lambda Literary Awards, and her manual on lesbian theater, *Take Stage! How to Direct and Produce a Lesbian Play*, was published in 1997 by Scarecrow Press. Her book of essays, *Like There's No Tomorrow: Meditations for Women Leaving Patriarchy*, was published in 1997 by Common Courage Press.

Sally Miller Gearhart is a recovering activist who lives on a mountain of contradictions in Northern California. She is the author of *The Wanderground* and coauthor of *A Feminist Tarot* and has published numerous short stories and articles. She appeared in the documentaries *The Times of Harvey Milk* and *Word Is Out*. She taught for forty years in academia and is now studying Spanish, barbershop harmony, tai chi chuan, New Age metaphysics, and a pit bull.

Elissa Goldberg's work has appeared in several anthologies and journals, including *Dykescapes, The Body of Love,* and *Bridges: A Jewish Feminist Journal.* Aside from writing and cooking, Elissa is a social worker who works with old people. She lives in Portland, Oregon.

Tzivia Gover is a freelance journalist whose work appears regularly in *The Boston Globe,* among other publications. Her poetry and prose have appeared in anthologies and journals, including *Family: A Celebration* (Peterson's), *My Lover Is a Woman: Contemporary Lesbian Love Poems* (Ballantine), *Sojourner,* and *The Evergreen Chronicles.* She has just completed a memoir and is currently writing a screenplay.

Carol Guess is the author of three novels, *Seeing Dell* (Cleis Press, 1996), *Switch* (Calyx Books, July 1998), and *Island a Strata* (Cleis Press, forthcoming).

Anndee Hochman's articles, essays, book reviews, and short fiction have been published in *The New York Times Book Review, The Philadelphia Inquirer, Ms.,* and *Philadelphia* magazine, among other places. Her book, *Everyday Acts & Small Subversions: Women Reinventing Family, Community and Home,* was published in 1994. She divides her time between Philadelphia and Portland, Oregon, the two homes where her heart lives.

Judy MacLean is a writer and editor in San Francisco. Her fiction has appeared in *Lesbian Love Stories: Volume 2, All the Ways Home: Parenting and Children in the Lesbian and Gay Communities,* and *Queer View Mirror.* Her humor pieces have appeared in *The Washington Post, San Francisco Chronicle, Dyke Life,* and *The Best Contemporary Women's Humor.* She is an activist for human rights; she backpacks, skis cross-country, and participates in mini triathlons.

Antonia Matthew was born in England and has lived in the United States since 1965. Her poetry has been published in magazines such as *Nimrod, California Quarterly,* and *Sistersong.* She was co-owner and comanager of Aquarius Books for a Feminist Future, in Bloomington, Indiana, until its closure in 1995.

Pam McArthur says, "I live in the Boston area with my beloved, Beth, and our son, Aaron. Thanks to Beth for inspiration. Thanks to Ginger Twist for support. And thanks to the muse, unpredictable though she is. About 'Sand Slip Away': The facts are fiction, but the spirit is true. Message from Marty to Rachel: Twelve years later, I still love you!"

Julie Mitchell, former bookseller and Angeleno, is currently on the road in search of her proverbial fortune.

Merril Mushroom is an old-timey dyke whose writing has been published in numerous anthologies and periodicals.

Deborah Schwartz is a poet by habit and nature, although she has slipped shamelessly into prose and is now completing her first novel, *Journeys Out From the Cage.* Most recently her work has been published in *Modern Words, G. W. Review, Aireings,* and *Sinister Wisdom.*

Anne Seale is a creator of lesbian songs, stories, and plays. Her tape of humorous lesbian songs, *Sex for Breakfast,* is available for $12 from Wildwater Records, P. O. Box 56, Webster, NY 14580. Her work has been or will soon be published in the anthologies *Ex-Lover Weird Shit, Pillow Talk, Life In a Day,* and in issues of the journal *Lesbian Short Fiction.*

Judith Stein is a fat Jewish lesbian who lives in Cambridge, Massachusetts, with her partner of fifteen years. A longtime political activist, Stein earns her living as a university administrator. She has had short stories and essays published in numerous journals and anthologies, including *Lesbian Love Stories* and *Lesbian Love Stories: Volume 2.* She is an editor and contributor to *All the Ways Home: Parenting and Children in the Lesbian and Gay Communities: A Collection of Short Fiction* (New Victoria, 1995).

Roey Thorpe lives in Ithaca, New York, where she was a city councilwoman for four years. Her stories have appeared in the following anthologies: *How To, Quickies: Lesbian Short-Shorts,* and *Lavender Mansions: 40 Contemporary Lesbian and Gay Short Stories.*

Uncumber's story, "The Birthday Party," was written a few years ago. Recently the author came out to her brother, other relatives, and some friends in the South. Their tolerant (although certainly not enthusiastic) acceptance of this news is, she believes, due to the mighty efforts of gay rights groups all over the country and to the work of media pioneers such as Deb Price, Lily Tomlin/ Jane Wagner, and Ellen Degeneres.

Jess Wells has had seven volumes of work published, including the novel *AfterShocks,* a collection of stories titled *Two Willow Chairs,* and an anthology, *Lesbians Raising Sons.* Her work has appeared in nearly two dozen literary anthologies, including *Women on Women, The Femme Mystique, Lavender Mansions, Lesbian Culture,* and *When I Am an Old Woman I Shall Wear Purple.* "The Common Price of Passion" is excerpted from a novel of the same title.

Julia Willis is the author of *Who Wears the Tux?, We Oughta Be in Pictures,* and the cat baby book *Meow-Mories.* Her novel, *Reel Time,* will be published by Alyson in 1998. She dedicates the story

"Swing Shift" to the memory of Rebecca Torrence.

Barbara Wilson's most recent novel is *If You Had a Family* (Seal Press). Her childhood memoir, *Blue Windows,* was published in 1997 (Picador USA). "Wood" is based on the tale "Frau Trude" from *Grimm's Fairy Tales.* She lives in Seattle.